Cabin Fever

Cabin Fever

Life Goes On in the Northwoods

Mike Lein

Jackpine Writers' Bloc, Inc.
Menahga, Minnesota 56464

Other Books by Mike Lein

Firewood Happens
Life, Liberty, and the Pursuit of Happiness in Minnesota's Northwoods

A simple book about the simple life. Winner of the Midwest Independent Publishers Association's 2016 Award for "Humor."

Down At The Dock
More Stories of the Good Life in the Northwoods

Life at the cabin gets more complicated. A look at serious subjects such as Bigfoot, skinny-dipping, and firewood theft. Winner of the Midwest Independent Publishers Association's 2017 Award for "Humor."

The Crooked Lake Chronicles
Mostly True Stories of Life Up North

Lightly embellished tales of the things that happen, the people you meet, and the struggles with Mother Nature that occur when you enjoy the simple life in the Great Outdoors. Finalist for the Midwest Independent Publishers Association's 2019 Award for "Humor."

All illustrations and cover artwork contributed
by Erik Espeland.

©Copyright 2021 Jackpine Writers' Bloc, Inc.
Jackpine Writers' Bloc, Inc., Publisher
13320 149th Ave
Menahga, MN 56464

2021 Mike Lein, All Rights Reserved.
Printed in the United States of America
ISBN # 978-1-928690-47-4
First Paperback Edition

Acknowledgments

I didn't think I was going to do a fourth "Northwoods Cabin" book this soon. With a trilogy of these already under my writer's belt, I planned on moving on to a few other books that were lying around deep inside the computer at various stages of development. But sometimes I'm wrong. "Cabin Fever" just sorta happened, a project born by the stories that kept happening, requests from readers, book sales, and having too much writing time on my hands while locked down during a pandemic.

As usual, this book couldn't have happened without the family, friends, and acquaintances who provide much of the fodder for the stories. Or the scenic and wild places that surround the cabin and other story locations. I salute you! Keep up the good work and please accept my apologies if you don't like my version of the story. I'll serve you up a beverage of your choice on the cabin deck and we'll talk about it.

This book would also not have been possible without my friends at the Jackpine Writers' Bloc. Sharon Harris keeps my Freshman English punctuation, and sometimes my grammar, within acceptable standards. Tarah Wolff formats the mess and figures out what the printer needs to get both the physical book and the e-book into the hands or electronics of readers. Before all this stuff happens, the active members of the writers' group suffer through readings of drafts of the stories and offer constructive ideas and comments to polish them up.

Erik Espeland of Field Hands takes the book theme and story ideas and turns them into a cover painting worth framing and individual chapter sketches to set the mood.

Without him, my books would not have that rustic, homegrown look and feel that I'm looking for. His work has been featured in all four books. Hopefully we both have more work to do.

So get to reading! Enjoy! Let me know if you want more. I'll keep wandering around "Up North" and we'll see what happens.

Notes:

The stories "Hooked" and "The Locals" were previously published in edited form in *The Talking Stick,* a publication of the Jackpine Writers' Bloc.

"Going Home" by Jim Lein was previously published in *Colorado Serenity* magazine located in Evergreen, Colorado.

Table of Contents

Foreword—The Beginning

I was sitting at the cabin's kitchen table on Super Bowl night, listening to the big game on an old school AM radio channel, when the name for this book came to me. I couldn't get the game on any of the three and a half channels the cabin TV brings in and I didn't really care. I had a snack tray full of sausage, cheese, and olives, and a 500-ml mini-box of cheap red wine. That's one way of dealing with cabin fever.

It had already been a rewarding winter trip to the cabin. The night before, I volunteered at Itasca State Park, helping at one of their winter events: a lantern-lit snowshoe hike through the pines out to Schoolcraft Point. I volunteer at these things for several reasons. One is that deep sense of civic responsibility instilled in me by my parents and others associated with the Western Minnesota Scandinavian culture I was born into. Another more "official" reason is to score volunteer hours needed to keep my Minnesota Master Naturalist title. I'll admit I sometimes come up a little short on the yearly forty hours of volunteer work needed. So, why not get started early for once? And besides civic duty and record-keeping, it got me outside on a winter night.

I can't think of a better way to beat cabin fever. More than two hundred fellow hardy Minnesotans of all ages, and a few from other lands such as Wisconsin and Iowa, showed up and went stomping along on snowshoes for over a mile-long hike beneath a silver half-moon and the brightest stars you have ever seen. Most of the crowd stopped back at the trailhead after the hike to roast marshmallows over a campfire safely stoked by another volunteer. Some even brought their hotdogs and had a family picnic in the great outdoors, under the stars, at twenty-five degrees, in January.

January had been a dark and gloomy month. But the skies cleared for this event. A couple of other volunteers and I hung out far down the trail, ready with free advice, words of encouragement, and flashlights and radios should any more serious help be needed. In reality, these folks needed little more than a few adjustments to snowshoe bindings and information on how much farther it was to the end point. I did hear a few "Are we there yet?" questions from old and young alike, but no regrets about the surroundings or the experience.

I ended the night by myself, the last one out on the trail, taking my time slowly shuffling snowshoes through the forest, stopping in clearings surrounded with snow-flocked pines, enjoying the silence of the night and the stars and the moon at my own pace.

As I sat back at the cabin the next night, at my private Super Bowl sausage-wine-cheese party, I sensed I was a lucky man, and that even though there was much more winter to come, I was well on the way to beating cabin fever. At least for this year. At least for 2020.

Well, I guess I got that wrong.

At the time there were reports out of China and a few closer places regarding a havoc-wreaking virus. Even though I had been trained in these types of things for almost forty years of professional life in the environmental protection/public health field, I didn't anticipate what was ahead of us. The pain, suffering, and death. The economic toll on the nation, friends, and family. And the lockdown. Forced isolation from those friends, family, and community. A whole new kind and level of cabin fever.

One friend made a statement to me that I won't forget. "Mike," he said, "this must be easy for you. While the rest of us are trapped in our homes, you have the great outdoors to roam, hunting and fishing. And you've got the cabin to hunker down in and write."

That was true in some ways. The cabin was a peaceful retreat once we got through the spring lockdown. But like many people, I spent most of that time at home, in our little house, trying to respect the public health officials that I had worked with for almost forty years. Respecting all my training that predicted emergencies like this.

So, I weathered the lockdown with Marcie and the dogs, each of us pointing out the other's irritating little habits. Like crunching corn flakes at breakfast. Reading every last word of the front page section of the newspaper before surrendering it. Not putting dishes in the dishwasher. Snoring. Hogging the computer all day. That water on the bathroom floor after every shower. Begging for one more treat. Demanding one more ball toss.

We survived. And to make the obvious perfectly clear, we are both thankful this was all we had to endure. Many other families all across our small world suffered through much worse and I'm sure those impacts aren't over.

My friend was right about one thing. The lockdown was great for writing, especially about the things I was missing. I'll leave the more serious stuff to other people, responsible media, and authors better suited to document it. Hopefully *Cabin Fever* does provide a look at the lighter side of life and serves as a well-earned escape and distraction.

But before we move on to the fun, I'd like to salute all the people who have so far assisted the human race and Planet Earth in getting through this. Whether you be a health care provider on the front lines, a grocery store or convenience store clerk keeping necessities flowing, or just another person who heeded common sense and the official recommendations that helped slow and contain the spread, you're all heroes to me!

Cabin Fever

Cabin Fever

Winter mornings at the cabin usually begin as calm and peaceful. The coffee pot starts perking, the dog (or dogs) are fed, and the fire relit in the wood stove. Maybe some bacon is fried up or some oatmeal heated to get the day going. Then comes time to sit at the table, watching the morning unfold outside windows framed in frost.

The bird feeders are the focus of nearby activity. There will be woodpeckers in the eye-level suet basket, everything from the small fluffy downy to the big prehistoric-looking pileated, all jockeying for position and territorial rights over the suet scraps. In contrast, the sunflower and thistle seed feeders will be busy with gold and purple finches stacked above each other, enjoying a communal meal and each other's company without squabbling. The old standbys, chickadees and nuthatches, will be flitting down to grab just one seed, then dart back to a safe perch to hammer it open and enjoy the good stuff.

There isn't usually much happening down the wooded hillside or out on the lake. Occasionally a deer or coyote will walk by on the remains of the old resort road, using it as a wildlife highway. Or a squirrel might pop out of a hole in a rotting aspen and bask in the early morning sun before heading uphill to raid the bird feeders. On a good morning, with the right mix of clouds hanging to the east, the sunrise steals the show, painting a purple and rose Northwoods picture through the trees, then breaking through to light the view below in bright gold. Every ripple or imperfection in the clean white page of the frozen lake casts its own shadow, big and small, revealing details that won't be visible once the sun climbs higher and the glare blurs details. The shadows from the island pine trees march back towards the sun as the day unfolds.

I could say that none of this ever gets old. Then again I'm mostly a nonfiction writer who writes about personal experiences and tries not to embellish them much. So here's the truth: Staring out a cabin window, in the depths of a long cold winter, does not protect you from that age-old malady known as "cabin fever." I'm assuming most readers are well aware of the term and the symptoms, so I won't linger long here. We all know what happens to our psyches after too many days trapped inside during dreary Minnesota winters.

The cure for cabin fever is simple, supposedly. Just get out there and enjoy nature or share some human companionship—just do something. That isn't always as simple or safe as it sounds, at least here in the cold northern climates. Have you ever read the short story "To Build a Fire" by Jack London? Jack Who? Come on now —just think *The Call of the Wild* or *White Fang* and if those two titles don't jog your memory, there's a lot of reading material and a couple of movies to catch up on.

The most famous version of "To Build a Fire" was published in 1908. It is fiction, but I'm betting Mr. London had plenty of true stories to pull material from.

Cabin Fever

I'm not going to give away the whole story or any spoilers—just set the stage. A Yukon Territory backwoodsman decides to explore some new country in the middle of a long cold winter. He's new to the country. This is his first winter there. Against the advice of an old timer, he splits from his partners and sets off with his dog in spite of the fact that it's well over fifty degrees below zero. He's confident he can hike down the river, check out some logging territory, and reunite with "the boys," as he calls them, at their camp by nightfall. He'll even stop along the way "to build a fire" and have lunch. What can go wrong?

Now I don't live at the cabin for long periods of time in the winter. However, cabin fever can become a problem even on a short visit when the ice fishing is poor, snow is too deep to hike the forest, and interior projects get boring. All of those recently came together.

I'd been at the cabin for a few days. Snow was piled feet deep around the yard and in the woods. I ran out of materials for interior projects. The slush and snow on the lake limited ice fishing opportunities and the dog was getting restless. Bored with watching bird feeders and needing some exercise, I set out to recreate "To Build a Fire." How would I do in this situation?

Unlike the conditions facing the man in the original story, it wasn't over fifty degrees below outside. It was in the low teens above zero. So think of that. More than sixty-five degrees warmer and it was still chilly. I also wasn't going to be walking a river many miles from civilization and there would be a state-of-the-art smartphone in my pocket and an emergency satellite locator device in my backpack. So you might say I had some advantages. I tried to cancel out some of these advantages by limiting fire-making utensils to a flint and steel. My plan was to hike halfway around the lake, stop at Duck Island "to build a fire," have a snack, and then continue on around the shore.

I pulled on my modern-day synthetic/wool-blend long underwear, insulated pants, and jacket. Then I put Sage's neoprene doggie vest on her for the walk. Now what do you suppose Jack London or his story's character would have thought about that? In her defense, she's a Labrador retriever, not the native sled dog-type featured in the story. Then we were off, stepping carefully down the hillside through a foot of snow and out onto Crooked Lake.

The off-shore portion of the lake was treacherous with slush pockets and crusted drifts and not nearly as interesting as the shoreline. There mink, otter, and fisher tracks showed that life in the frigid outdoors continued on despite the long winter. The dog and I crunched across the channel to Big Island and followed the irregular shore. Sage was happy to be free of the confines of the cabin and the snow bank-encircled yard. She loped ahead of me in bird-dog fashion, making short trips into the grass and brush on shore, then veering out onto the open lake, checking out any interesting pine cone or branch that winter winds had sent skating across the ice. Just past the leaning pine tree, she made a dash up the snowless south bank of the island, nose to the air, and flushed three ruffed grouse who had been basking in the morning sun.

I called her back and we continued up the shore, checking out the otter slides on the north-facing slopes and the piles of animal scat perched on exposed shoreline rocks. Apparently a rock makes a comfortable winter toilet for mink and fisher . . .

About three quarters of a mile from the cabin, we crossed the narrow channel to our destination. Duck Island is a local name that won't be found on any maps of the surrounding state forest. It's actually an archipelago or chain of three small pine-covered islands, attached by strips of swampy grass with just enough water to wet your feet if stepping across during open water seasons. One island contains a rock firepit and a comfortable log bench set in stately white pines with a scenic overlook of the lake. It was here I planned to conduct my fire-making experiment and celebrate with a fire-roasted venison sausage for an outdoor lunch.

The best-laid plans started to go bad at this point. Those stately white pines surrounding the firepit had shaded the ground from the warming, melting rays of the sun. The firepit and log bench were buried under a foot and a half of snow. It was a tough trek uphill through the snow to discover this. Sage was smarter. She refused to make the trip, hanging back on the lake, staring at me, trying to figure out what this stupid human was doing this time. I might mention that the dog in "To Build a Fire" had similar doubts about things his human did in that story.

So I gave up on my scenic firepit plan and

stomped back out through the snow to the lake, now perspiring from the effort. That was only a minor problem for me. But that Yukon adventurer probably didn't have damp-wicking, warm-when-wet insulated clothing. I searched farther down the shore and found a snow-free grassy area on a sunny point. Sage approved, grabbed a stick, and demanded to play a game of fetch while I started the fire-making experiment.

The story's character had matches to try to start his fire. Some type of fire-making match has been around for hundreds of years. The Chinese likely had them well over a thousand years ago, with Western cultures developing a series of different forms, some dangerous and poisonous, starting in the early to mid-1800s. My flint and steel were something an earlier fur trapper or voyageur exploring this neck of the woods might have used.

Making a fire with flint and steel involves banging a piece of the right sharp rock, flint in this case, against the right type of steel. If done correctly, it creates a shower of sparks. The sparks are actually tiny pieces of flaming metal, scraped from the steel and heated by the friction of the action. The sparks fall into a pre-prepared nest of flammable tinder to create small smoking embers. The embers are encouraged to grow into flames by aggressively blowing on them and the tinder. Increasingly large twigs and sticks are added to the flames until the right size campfire is created. Simple enough—right?

I retrieved my flint and steel from the backpack and got started. My steel was a hand-forged horseshoe-shaped piece reproduced to resemble one from American colonial history. The flint was a flat piece of flint rock, about two inches by three inches, sharpened by chipping off (napping) small pieces of the stone around the edges. This creates a very sharp-edged rock that can also be used as a small knife or scraper if needed.

Like any well-prepared early adventurer, I carried tinder material in the form of charred wood bits in a small tin box about the size of a chewing tobacco container. I made a nest of dry grass while Sage continued to drop the stick at my feet, demanding attention and some retrieving action. I started banging the flint against the steel, showering sparks into the box of char. I got success with only a few strikes. A tiny red ember started glowing and smoking on a piece of charred wood. I quickly transferred it to the grass tinder and blew. Instant flames! I sat back to gloat—and then watched the dry grass burn up and extinguish before I could scramble to add more lasting material.

I got better prepared for round two, stockpiling tiny dry twigs and small bits of broken branches to feed the initial blaze, before starting the sparking process. I'd only done this a few times before and it appeared that I got lucky on that first try. This time it took several minutes of striking the flint against the steel before I got a glowing ember, transferred it to the tinder nest, and blew like I was trying to extinguish birthday candles. Flames quickly appeared but my lack of experience showed again. The twigs and broken branches were stubborn to light and the flames died out while I frantically searched for more ignitable matter.

Okay—round three. By this time I was getting frustrated and my hands were cold and numb. Let's again consider what this process would have been like if it were fifty degrees below zero and maybe I was soaked from a fall through the ice. Even with matches, it might be a challenge to build a sizable campfire. And then there was Sage, demanding attention with her stick, not knowing that there was a sausage treat if the fire ever got going.

Nearby was the friend of every fire-maker in the Northwoods. A dead birch tree with dry branches and peeling bark stood rotting away just up the shore. I collected a bunch of increasingly larger branches and stripped off several rolls of paper-like white bark. Since this tree was already dead, stripping the bark did no damage. Don't try this on a live tree!

Once again I made a nest of dead grass, this time adding small curls of the highly ignitable birch bark. Striking a good spark into the char took longer than I would like to admit due to a dull flint and cold hands. But I eventually scored a glowing ember, moved it to the tinder nest, huffed and puffed until both the grass and bark ignited. This bundle of flames was carefully transferred to my potential campfire where both sticks and more birch bark awaited. I then sat back and added bigger sticks as the small fire grew until I had a sausage-roasting, hand-warming blaze going.

Sage took a time-out from her stick game when the sausage came out of the pack, standing by drooling and waiting for her share as it toasted to a golden brown over the campfire. Lunch never tasted so good!

Cabin Fever

I enjoyed the fire as it burned down before extinguishing it with the ample snow nearby. Then Sage and I continued our hike off around the bay. My arm would be sore from throwing her stick by the time we got back to the cabin. But I learned a few things about how "to build a fire," was warm and dry, and had cured cabin fever for the day. Let's just say that's way better than the guy in Mr. London's story fared.

A Room With a View

Many people, including other writers, often ask me why I choose to write "creative non-fiction," or in other words, mostly true stuff. There seems to be a subtle bias in their questioning. Like only "fiction" writers," or "liars" as I call them, are true writers. In my defense, I always point out that I have on occasion joined the Liars Club and written some award-winning fiction. But I also always finish with the line that "truth is stranger than fiction—and a whole lot funnier."

So let's look at an example. Any reader of my previous stuff will know that I'm not afraid to hand out advice or voice my opinions when it comes to life at the cabin or what a real cabin should look like or have for amenities. Any real cabin should have a wood stove and some sort of wood exterior—no fake electric or gas "wood" stoves or fireplaces for me. I'll also take the real log siding on the exterior, if you please. Who ever thought up that vinyl log siding? That stuff ought to be illegal! But let's move on past that and get to bathrooms.

Our cabin infamously still has an outhouse for the main bathroom facility. It's made of real plywood and has a door. Pretty standard you might think, even for an outhouse. Well, not always. Anyone who has traveled to the paradise we Minnesotans call the Boundary Waters Canoe Area Wilderness knows that the bathrooms there are pretty primitive. They are usually screened from the campsite by natural vegetation but that's it. No walls. No windows. No doors. Just a wide-open magnificent view of the wilderness lake you just canoed. So there are exceptions.

However, there are also apparently exemptions to this rule for recreational homes and cabins. Maybe it's a new trend. Maybe I'm just old-fashioned. Maybe I'm just not hip or cool no more. But I find this trend somewhat disturbing, even for one who is not necessarily known for his modesty.

So here's the deal. About forty-five years ago I pulled up to the college dormitory in my red 1969 Chevy Camaro with the black racing stripes and shiny chrome mag wheels. Yes, I was cool way back then. I saw my friend Patty walking down the sidewalk with another girl and waved her over.

"Mikie," she said (she always calls me Mikie), "this is Marcie. How about giving us a ride to the ice cream shop?"

Now what cool guy in a red Chevy Camaro is going to say "No" to that? Patty crawled into the tight back seat and let Marcie and me get acquainted on the short ride. She's sneaky like that. It wasn't exactly love at first sight but forty-five years later we still are married, perhaps in spite of the outhouse at the cabin. See how I brought that back around to bathrooms there?

Anyway, we all graduated from college, agreed to stay in touch, and did. Just about every year thereafter, Patty and her husband Dave, my one-time roommate Kim and his wife Annette, and Marcie and I, take a short trip in

February or March. It usually has been to a hotel in a city within driving distance of everyone. Nothing fancy. Just a short break from the winter and cabin fever. A long weekend spent relaxing in a hotel hot tub, shopping, eating, and drinking a few things. But a few years ago, near the end of a long cold winter, we all decided we could do better. Like getting-on-an-airplane-and-spending-a-week-in-a-warm-sunny-place better. The snowbird thing. A real break from cabin fever.

So the ladies did some planning, and late in February we all met at the airport and took an airplane ride to Arizona. Since we all live on or near and like to play on the water, the location had "lake" in its name and the accommodations were a recreational home near a lake. I won't call it a lake cabin even though it had a wood fireplace. It was too big, had stucco for siding, and it had air conditioning.

It did have three indoor bathrooms, one for every couple. An indoor bathroom is something Marcie likes on a vacation and something the other ladies weren't willing to do without. Now here is where we get to the truth-is-stranger-than-fiction part. One of the bedrooms was huge with a walk-in closet, likely what you would call the Master Suite. It also had what those house-hunting and remodeling TV shows call an "on-suite" bathroom. And what an on-suite bathroom it was! A tub, his and her sinks, double raindrop shower heads (which I didn't even know existed), and the usual throne. Everything Marcie would like to have in her cabin bathroom once it gets built. Except for one thing. Except for the view.

Cabin Fever

This was not the view expected from a vacation home. Not a view of majestic snowcapped mountains. Not a view of a simmering sun-kissed lake with a sandy beach and a lawn chair beckoning you to get outside. The entire wall facing the bedroom was made of very clear unfrosted glass. Glass so clear you had to feel for it as you approached to figure out where the door ought to be.

Forgive me, but let's make this perfectly clear. In this bedroom, it was entirely possible to lay on the big king-sized bed, right in front of the glass bathroom, and look through the perfectly clear clean glass wall right into the shower just a couple feet from the bed. You also had an unobstructed view of the sinks and the throne. So to make things even clearer, you could lie on the bed and watch your partner—or whoever else was in the bathroom—do whatever and all they were doing in the bathroom. I hope you don't need a clearer picture than that.

Now maybe I have changed from that cool guy in the red Camaro back then to an old fuddy-duddy or whatever the term is today. But I call that bathroom just plain weird and so did the rest of our crew. I might not mind a bathroom with a view when camping out in the Boundary Waters. I might even leave the cabin's outhouse door open if it's a pretty spring day with the birds singing, the chipmunks playing, and the loons calling. But it ain't happening if anyone else is around, as much for my respect for their eyes as it is out of what little modesty I have. So don't go expecting me to recommend construction of glass outhouses at cabins or actually installing glass bathroom walls in the tight confines of our own little cabin. Now we were stuck in this place for a week. It was already paid for and the rest of the place wasn't that bad. So we had to make a decision who got the glass bathroom suite. That turned out to be easy. We added the ages of each husband and wife couple together and divided by two. The couple with the lowest average age won. That was Kim and Annette in this case and they didn't object.

Maybe, as the youngsters of the group, they could appreciate the ambiance of the glass bathroom. Maybe they would enjoy the view. The rest of us old people will just keep on wondering what the architect or owner was fantasizing about when they planned this place. We probably won't solve that mystery. I don't think any of us are that cool anymore.

Hooked

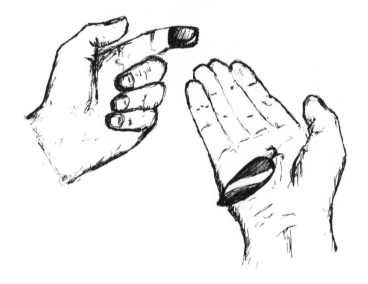

Hooked

I'm not one of those guys who picks a summer fishing spot by heading towards the nearest concentration of fishing boats. Likewise, when ice fishing, I tend to pick a remote lake or at least a remote corner of a lake, far away from the maddening crowd of fancy wheeled fish houses, buzzing ATVs, roaring ice augers, and one-ton pickups that make the ice crack and groan as they roll past. I like the solitude, the quiet, and an unencumbered view out my frosty windows.

So today I parked my pickup near the shore of a small lake and followed the lead of my GPS to a spot it knew at the opposite end. I'd had good luck there before and assumed fish still lived in the general area. Two holes drilled with a hand auger, the insulated portable fish house unfolded from a case and popped over the holes, and there you have it—fishing in my own private spot with only my own private thoughts and hopefully a fish or two to break up the solitude.

I started catching little perch right away. Small six-inch babies that were unhooked and sent back down the hole to swim until the same time next year. It was a good sign. Maybe the bigger perch and even a few crappies would cruise over to see what the action was about. Before that could happen, my line twitched again and one more small perch was cranked up through the ice hole. It was hooked lightly in the corner of the mouth by the small set of treble hooks on the jigging spoon and was bending my light little rod in a bowed arc. As my left hand stretched out to greet it, the perch gave one last midair flop. The hook pulled out and the bent fiberglass rod sent the treble hook zooming upwards towards my hand like an arrow shot from a bow.

One of the three extremely sharp little hooks nailed me right in the left hand pinky finger and buried itself to the hilt. This was not immediately painful. After all, it was a small hook, barely a quarter of an inch across from the point to the shank, not some huge honking muskie hook. I looked at it with disgust, pushed the floppy perch back down the hole with a boot, and considered options.

There are four hook-removal techniques that I am aware of. Three are doctor-approved. I've used three of the four a time or two over the years. I'll spare you the gruesome details of those incidents for now. Let's just say none are absolutely painless.

The non-doctor-approved method is what I call the "Grip it, Rip it, and Scream." This is probably the most commonly used one, practiced by most brave manly fishermen. First you grip the hook with a pliers, usually a rusty one that was rattling around in the bilge of the boat for a couple of years. You then grit your teeth, or bite down on a stick, or clamp a bullet between your teeth like the cowboys in those old Western movies, and rip the hook back out the way it came. Now you scream in pain as the hook's barb catches a few sensitive nerves on the way out. Like I said, this method is not doctor-approved but us tough guys rarely follow doctors' advice whether it be for diet, drinking, or hook removal. Naturally this was the method I tried first. I dug around in my fishing gear backpack and found a small multi-tool. One of those cheap combination knife-screwdriver-nail clipper-pliers models you get free for renewing your membership in some conservation organization or for spending a thousand dollars at a big box sporting goods store. I folded the tiny pliers out of it and considered it with doubt but went ahead with the operation. I grabbed that little hook, gritted my teeth, and gave it a hard yank. Yes, I screamed—and cursed very loudly. It seems that even little barbed perch hooks have real good hooking power. It didn't budge. It did find some very sensitive nerves.

I stuck my hand in the ice hole to numb the pain while considering the next three options. These are the doctor-approved options. The last one any of us manly fishermen will use, and the most drastic, involves actually driving to a doctor's office or medical clinic to seek professional help. There was no way I was going to do that for just a tiny little perch hook. I'd be the laughing stock of the medical community. My fishing buddies were sure to find out and mock me for years. It's also true that I would surely still scream in pain once I saw the doctor's bill for removing a tiny little perch hook.

So I moved on to the second doctor option. I call this one the "Loop It, Rip It, and Scream" method. It involves wrapping a loop of fishing line around the hook, apply downward pressure on the hook shank and pulling hard in the opposite direction—while screaming in pain. The theory is that the combination of pressure and pulling on the line loop will send the hook back out the channel it made without further damage.

Here I found one disadvantage of fishing alone. It's hard to perform this operation by yourself one-handed. I struggled to get a line loop under the hook. I finally managed to do that, then awkwardly pressed down on the hook shank with a thumb, gritted my teeth once again, and jerked back hard on the line in the direction I hoped the hook had gone in. No luck here either. After I stopped screaming and shoved my hand back down the ice hole for pain relief, nothing had been accomplished other than finding some new sensitive nerve endings in the hooked pinky finger.

I was rapidly running out of options other than the doctor visit. The last known hook removal technique is what I call the "Push It, Scream, and Clip It." The medical community actually formally refers to this one as the "Advance and Cut" method, in case you wonder about that type of thing. Note that "Scream" has been moved up to the second spot in the steps of this procedure. In this case, these steps are much more painful than the removal itself. You grit your teeth or bite on your bullet, take a deep breath, push the pointed end of the hook farther into the wound and out into the open air of the other side of the finger, cheek or other involved body part. You scream for a while and curse a bit. Then clip the now exposed point and barb off the hook with the wire cutter from that rusty pliers and pull the remains of the hook back out the entrance wound.

I hoped that my finger was sufficiently numb from its ice water bath to perform this operation. I grabbed the hook shank with my little multi-tool pliers, gritted my teeth, and gave it a twisting push to force the point out the backside of the finger. It took a couple tries. The finger was not as numb as I hoped. There was some screaming and cursing involved. In the end, I was successful with this step as both the point and barb of the hook were exposed. I was also more firmly hooked than before and that cheap little multi-tool pliers refused to clip the hook which was apparently made with some space-age metal.

What now? Was it time to admit defeat and take a painful drive to the doctor's office with a hook dangling from my hand? Time to endure further pain, mockery and a painfully large medical bill for professional help?

I dug once more into my messy backpack of fishing supplies, rooting around for a solution. There, hidden in a bottom corner under snacks, beer, and small electronic gizmos, was the heavy-duty fishing pliers with the side-cutting wire snips I should have found long before messing around with the little multi-tool. The final steps were anticlimactic after all the drama, screaming, and cursing. I clipped the point and barb off and wormed the remaining parts of the hook backwards out of the pinky with just a few small screams.

I then packed up my gear, folded up the fish house, and set back off for the truck. I was fishless but at least all my body parts were intact. I considered my ice fishing methods on the long walk. Fishing alone in a remote spot obviously has disadvantages when accidents like this happen. The operation would have been quicker and perhaps less painful with help from a companion. Then again, out here alone on the desolate ice of a remote lake, there's no nosy neighbors to hear you scream.

The Locals

The Locals

The door of the Buckhorn Bar swung open, allowing a blast of fresh below-zero backwoods air to sweep down my side of the bar. The crowd sitting on the far side, JR, Beans, Tiny, and Donnie, swung their heads in unison, looking up from warming shorty tap beers to see what else came with it.

Four kids followed the cold blast in, quickly slamming the door behind them before taking time to survey the surroundings. Two couples, it looked like, maybe in their thirties but hard to say given the shiny puffy coats and faux fur hats. Each one clutched a smartphone and now surveyed the tight confines of the Buckhorn with apprehension growing in wide eyes, suddenly aware of the atmosphere—and the silence—that greeted them.

It was a classic stare-down, like one of those from a bad old Western movie. Someone had to make a move, say the first word. One of the guys finally appointed himself "Leader" and walked forward to the bar. The others hung back, nervously looking up from their phones at JR, Beans, Tiny, and Donnie, the ratty stuffed moose head hanging on the wall above them, and the ancient stuffed and badly varnished muskie decaying below it. Then one of the ladies noticed Big Louie, whispering to the others and pointing with a mixture best described as surprise and horror.

Big Louie sat in an old webbed lawn chair on a shelf above the fuzzy TV tuned to a hockey game in progress. He had been a clothing store mannequin in a former life. Where, nobody could really remember. There was speculation he was a garage sale purchase dating back to the early '70s. He now watched over the crowd, beady eyes peering out from under a hillbilly-style floppy felt hat. While he maybe sported some high fashion duds in his former employment, bibs and lumberjack plaid were the current uniform. And that's not all. Lying across his lap was a rusty old double-barrel shotgun. The shotgun remained clutched in his cold plastic hands, pointed towards the far wall—for now.

Bull finished shoving a couple hunks of oak into the blazing fireplace, closed the screen and walked back to reclaim his throne behind the bar. He took a sip of his own beer and stared back at Leader Guy, waiting. We all watched and kept our mouths shut, anticipating what was going down next.

Leader Guy blinked and went first—"Aaahhh, hi there. We're out looking for my sister. We were supposed to meet her at the place down the road but she didn't show up. We thought she might have stopped in here. You guys seen her?"

Bull took another sip of his beer. "Nope," he said, not bothering to ask for a description. After all, a lone female stepping into the Buckhorn late on a winter Saturday night would have been an event talked about for years. We kept these thoughts to ourselves and let Bull do the talking.

The Locals

"Well, okay," said Leader Guy, glancing back at his uneasy followers, still nervously scrolling their phones, glancing up once in a while to keep an eye on Big Louie. "Maybe she will show up. We might as well have a drink. You got any 'Fireball' whiskey?"

"Nope," said Bull, not even bothering to point to the meager row of half-full bottles of Jack, Jim, Canadian, and Crown on the shelf behind him.

Leader Guy didn't give up. "How about some 'Hot 100'?" he asked.

"Nope," said Bull, again letting the bottles behind him speak for themselves.

Leader Guy seemed slow to take a hint. "Well, aaahh, got anything with some cinnamon in it to warm us up?"

"Nope," said Bull, sticking to his story.

Leader Guy finally wised up, looked down at his own phone, fumbled to check something, then started a slow walk backwards to the rest of his group, still standing only one step into the Buckhorn. "Well, okay then, I guess we should keep on looking for my sister, don't know where she might have went, might have to run back to the cabin and check there, let her know we are looking for her if she shows up, thanks for the information and have a good night."

Bull nodded in return as the group hurried back through the door, trying to cram through two at a time, again filling the Buckhorn with a quick blast of cold country air. Silence reigned, the only sounds that of the oak crackling in the fireplace, one log rolling forward with a thud to press against the screen. Bull took a short sip of beer, stood up, and walked back across the crooked unvarnished floor to poke the log back into place.

I tilted my empty glass at him as he came back. He refilled it with bubbly golden goodness from the tap and scratched around in the remains of the twenty lying on the bar in front of me. The wordless transaction having gone down without a hitch, and things being kinda slow on my side of the bar, I picked up the glass and walked over to the other side to see what wisdom could be found there.

Donnie greeted me with a laugh and a "Hey, Mike, how's the fishing been?"

Before I could answer, he looked down the row of occupied bar stools to his left and got the conversation rolling like he always does. "Hey guys, remember that night back in the '70s? The night we had the lottery? A buck a chance to shoot the TV when Howard Cosell came on Monday Night Football! That Son-Of-A-Bitch just hated the Vikings! Tiny—you won the lottery, didn't you? Damn, that was crazy! You musta made a hundred bucks and I bet ol' Louie is still deaf!"

The Snowplow Fairy

The Snowplow Fairy

When you live in the Far North, snow removal is a big deal. How's that for an understatement? And since it's such a big deal, there's a lot of pride that goes with being a manly man and being able to deal with snow in an effective and professional manner. Now I know many women do deal in snow removal out of necessity and pride. But they don't seem to view it with the same intensity that comes with the male ego. If a woman hires someone to remove their snow, it's likely to be viewed as a very practical solution for her. A healthy man would likely be viewed as weak or lazy and ridiculed throughout his neighborhood for the same offense.

I risked this fate in the aftermath of the last snow storm while at home in our small town. I decided to let the current "blizzard-like conditions" run their course before firing up my big ol' 10-horse snow blower. I got out of bed, put on some decent clothes, and blasted the four-wheel-drive truck out the driveway and through the plow drift to go to church. That civic duty completed, I blasted back into the garage, made Marcie and the dogs breakfast, and was enjoying the paper and my third cup of coffee when the neighborhood snowplow fairy showed up.

"Snowplow Fairy" is a local term as far as I know. However, I'm betting it's one that should be well understood by other North Country dwellers. I first heard it from a friend who told me about an anonymous guy who randomly shows up early on snowy mornings to quickly and efficiently plow their driveway. The mystery plow driver then moves on without asking for monetary compensation or any other reward. She and her husband were lying snug and warm in their bed on one such cold snowy morning, delaying rolling out to deal with the snow before heading to work. "Maybe the snowplow fairy will show up," one of them suggested.

In my case, I knew who the snowplow fairy was. It was a guy down the street who regularly gets his kicks out of using his John Deere snow blower to help out other neighbors. I don't mind this at all when we aren't home, or when Marcie is home alone. She can't handle the big manly beast of a snow-blowing machine that I keep in the storage shed. It is nice to come home from a trip to the cabin and find the snowplow fairy has visited and neatly plowed the driveway, thus giving me a clear path into the garage for the painful ordeal of unpacking. But here I was, home, drinking coffee in my easy chair, while some manlier man took care of my responsibility.

I quickly donned my arctic gear, rushed out to the storage shed and got the snow blower rolling in time to help finish. I even shoveled the front step with him watching, just so he realized I wasn't some old lazy guy who took his snow removal duties lightly. I gave him a thumbs-up over the roar of the blowers and then moved on to supervise snow removal activities at the neighbor's house across the street, just to further emphasis that I wasn't hiding in the house shirking duties or being a sissy about the weather.

I have also noticed through years of experience that snow removal is a subject that something like nine out of ten northern males have strong opinions on. They tend to feel they are experts in the field even though their experience is limited to a thirty-foot small-town driveway. This was never more evident than at the December meeting of the local sportsmen's club I belong to. It was one of those meetings where you look at the agenda and think "This should take about fifteen minutes and then I can pay my dues and be out of here in time for the hockey game."

It would have been except for the open-ended question the President threw out near what should have been the close of the meeting. "Guys," he said, "one of our members has been taking care of snow removal out here with his own equipment and time. I'm thinking we should budget for a skid-steer loader with a bucket and start taking care of it ourselves."

I looked around the room and inwardly, and maybe outwardly, groaned. Sitting around me in the rapidly overheating room were around seventy males of the species. Not a single reasonable woman in sight. Most were within ten or fifteen years of my age. I knew what that meant. Odds were that seated in this crowd were at least sixty-three experts in snow removal, each with his own expert opinion. Every one of those experts had just been given a blank check to share that expert opinion and weigh in on the faults of all the expert opinions of every other one of the experts who was about to voice his expert opinion.

And so it began. While I held my tongue and watched the clock on the wall tick away, expert after expert offered up opinions and took exception to the last stated expert opinion. There are many ways to accomplish snow removal, each with its own pluses and minuses. They were all roundly debated including buying a skid-steer loader, leasing a skid-steer loader, buying an old tractor at an auction, and asking a dealer to donate some sort of machine to the Club. The inability of other members to safely and effectively operate such machines was also argued at length. Even the unmanly option of hiring a snow removal service was voiced by a member and then quickly opposed as being unsustainably expensive—and unmanly.

The discussion was mercifully starting to wind down when a member suggested an obvious solution. Obvious to him anyway. "Why don't we just pay Joe to do what he's already doing?" I know I outwardly groaned at this suggestion. The guy next to me in the close confines of the now ninety-degree room looked at me suspiciously. Now here's why that was a bad idea, in my expert opinion.

Joe had obviously been serving as the Club's snowplow fairy. He was taking pride in doing a good job and doing it without pay or other compensation. For true snowplow fairies, this pride in a job well done, done under their own terms, and done with their own expert skills, is enough. Doubt me? Go ahead—try to pay your own snowplow fairy in cash should one show up in your driveway. A hot cup of coffee? Sure. A bag of fresh baked cookies—hell yes! Money? You just insulted him or her, damaged their pride, assumed that they expected monetary reward when they wanted nothing more than to do a good deed and perhaps pump up their reputation and self-esteem.

Joe was present and now weighed in. As expected, he proudly stated that even though it took many long hours, often in the dark of night, to manage the snow, he was happy to do so and to continue to do it! No compensation needed!

The meeting disintegrated into babble. Some other expert immediately offered up his expert legal opinion that the Club couldn't pay Joe because he was a member and the Club's non-profit status did not allow paying a member. Others started arguing the merits of their expert opinions with the expert sitting in the chair next to them. The President finally brought the meeting to a merciful close by pounding the gavel and promising to "look into it more." I think the hockey game was well into the second period by the time I got home and poured myself a stiff one.

So given all this, you might think that snow removal at the cabin is a complicated thing since there's nine hundred feet of driveway, a big yard and many feet of snow in a typical winter. Not really. A couple full-time neighbors take care of part of the shared driveway. For the rest, I've got my own Northwoods snowplow fairy in the form of neighbor Bill and his big old diesel-powered F350—"The White Stallion." Now Bill isn't your typical snowplow fairy. He does expect to be paid something for his effort given that the White Stallion is a thirsty beast. This isn't the church's parking lot after all. But he does take pride in his work. I have to recognize that.

He stopped over one pre-winter fall day to get the lay of the land and check in on the neighborhood gossip. He immediately noticed the shiny new red snowplow hanging off the front of my small beat-up ATV. He eyed it with suspicion from his seat high in the White Stallion and jumped to conclusions.

"Well," he said, "looks like you aren't going to be needing my services this year. I suppose you will try to plow your driveway with THAT!"

I could tell he was insulted, assuming that I, in my expert opinion, had decided that a small ATV with a cheap little plow could replace him, his years of snow-removal experience, and the White Stallion. I think the pickup even missed a beat or two with its hearty diesel-fueled rattle. Yes, even what you may think of as an inanimate piece of equipment can be insulted. Just try starting your outboard motor, lawn mower, or snow blower after insulting it with a few bad names.

"NO, NO, NO—hang on a second!" I quickly jumped in and cut off that line of thought. I walked over to my own truck, got out the checkbook, and came back.

I held out a check and tried to make things perfectly clear. "The ATV is for plowing roads on the lake out to the fish house. You are quick, cheap, and dependable. Why would I mess with that? Here's some upfront money for the next few months. Let me know

🐕

when you need more!"

Bill grinned, accepted the check, rolled up his window, and drove off, the White Stallion expressing their satisfaction and pride with a very manly rumble. I really dodged that bullet. Like my hero Clint Eastwood used to say in those old action movies—"A man's got to know his limitations."

Spring Fever

Spring Fever

Spring Fever. It's a lot like cabin fever. You've been stuck inside all winter long and now it's spring or almost spring, even if it's snowing while the sun is shining. The lakes might still be ice-covered but the grass is showing where the sun can reach it, the rhubarb has peeked out for a look at the weather, and maybe even the first frogs of spring are croaking in the swamp.

Spring fever has one other thing in common with cabin fever. It leads some of us guys to do stupid things in our haste to get out there and enjoy the fresh air. This can sometimes be written off to youth and testosterone. Like the time back in college when I drove my red Camaro down a forest road on a muddy spring day, looking to be the first guy back into a secret fishing hole.

For the unaware, a Camaro is meant to be a good-looking, low-slung sports car for driving fast on paved roads. They are never a good choice for a Minnesota winter/snow/mud vehicle unless you do one of those redneck things like jacking up the suspension about six feet and installing four-wheel drive. I made it to the lake all right, powering through a nasty mud hole with only two-wheel drive, shiny chrome mag wheels spinning and flinging mud, and bottoming out the frame due to the one-inch ground clearance. But something happened on the way back out. The mud hole got muddier or maybe I made it deeper on the way in. I buried that beautiful red

Camaro with shiny chrome mag wheels and black racing stripe deep into that spring mud hole.

This was way before cell phones. So I had no way to call my roommate with his four-wheel-drive truck to come to the rescue. In hindsight, I should have "borrowed" that truck for this trip. So I spent the next several hours using a proven mud hole extraction technique. Jack the car up out of the mud. Place branches, logs, and rocks under the wheels. Give er' hell, let the mud fly, and hope. Usually that gets about one or two feet of progress and then you repeat the process until said vehicle is out of the mud hole. It eventually worked and I headed back to our humble mobile home, broke-college student housing situation. Side note—this mobile home actually had bullet holes through its walls as a result of a disagreement amongst former tenants.

I hadn't known that I was on a schedule that day. It turns out I arrived well after I was supposed to be home. My roommate Dick was sitting in what passed as "the living room" in the front of the trailer, watching TV, and probably drinking a cheap beer. He refused to acknowledge my presence as I walked in, weary and mud-splattered from the ordeal. So I went back to my space, cleaned up, and returned to plop down near him and open my own cheap beer.

"Okay," I says. "So what's up with you?"

"Where the hell have you been?" he says back in a hurt voice. "You should have been home on time. I made pork chops."

Thus that trip taught me two valuable lessons.

One, watch what and where you are driving on muddy spring roads. The second lesson prepared me well for my future marriage. Don't be late for dinner. Sometimes these early lessons get lost on us guys. Especially when you get old enough to use a failing memory as an excuse. A year or so ago I got a bad case of spring fever. It was mid-April and spring should have arrived. The hillside down to the lake was snow-free but the lake was still frozen and there was snow deep in the forest, in the pines, where the sun never shines. The local authorities had not yet closed the forest roads to prevent road damage and stupidity. The roads were frozen solid and crusted over with snowmobile tracks. And besides, who needed to or would be dumb enough to drive on them this time of year anyway?

By now I had a state-of-the-art pickup truck with big tires and four-wheel drive. I'm not one of those "mudder" guys who go tearing up backcountry roads, pastures, and golf courses in my badass truck just for fun. But I do get into some pretty nasty situations now and then in pursuit of game, fish, and adventure. I like to be somewhat prepared.

I bid Marcie and the fluffy dog good-bye for the time being, put the truck in four-wheel drive, and headed down the nearest frozen forest road intent on scouting out the local turkey population and getting some exercise for me and the big dog. I drove a few miles back and pulled off the beaten path to park lest some other hearty traveler came by. The next few hours were spent hiking while looking for turkey tracks, enjoying the slow-awakening early-spring forest, and throwing a few sticks for Sage. We put on a few miles and then headed back to the truck as the sun sank toward the western horizon and hunger set in.

Drum roll please! Yes, I got stuck. The warming weather had turned the snow into a sugary, slippery mess that spun out from beneath the truck's tires and sank it in place. It was extremely frustrating. Many bad words were said. Thankfully Sage has heard them all before and chose to take a nap in the truck while I swore some more and pondered options.

The road was still hard-packed and passable, only a few feet away, taunting me. I could dig the tire jack out of the truck and use that old jack-up, put-logs-under-the-wheels, give-er'-hell, and repeat method. The trouble is, that method is much more difficult with a heavy-weight, full-sized pickup than a lightweight compact sports car, and, in this case, my use of the four-wheel drive option had buried four wheels, not two. It would be twice the work of hauling branches and logs, and jacking up the big truck. To further complicate matters, I had already taken the winter snow shovel out of the truck for some reason, maybe because it was supposed to be spring.

This time I did have a cell phone, so there were other options to consider. I could call for help. That is not as simple a decision as it may seem. Any man who's ever been in a situation like this knows that calling for help has consequences.

Calling back to the cabin to talk to Marcie and the fluffy dog would be futile. For one thing, they had no means to come and assist unless she was willing to walk several miles, with just a snow shovel and fluffy dog for protection, down a snow-packed forest road, probably in the dark, with coyotes and maybe even a few wolves howling in that dark forest. That was not going to happen. And besides, maybe I could get out of this without her ever finding out. Thus I would escape the ridicule associated with her pointing out my short-comings as an outdoorsman and me having to admit that I could make a dumb move once in a while.

Another option was to call a professional towing service. Somewhere some professional with a four-wheel-drive tow truck was waiting by the phone for someone like me to call. This option would have a heavy cost. He or she would take my credit card and ring up a good-sized charge for use of their equipment and expertise. To add to that cost, what if Marcie opened the credit card bill before I could waylay it and found out about both the incident and the cost? I'd pay for that. The tow truck operator was also likely to talk about this incident at the local coffee shop, municipal liquor store, church, or all three. "Shoulda seen the dumb move this old guy made up in the forest the other day! Luckily he had his cell phone and credit card with him."

Maybe I'd have to do that. First, there was one other possible option. My neighbor Marv has a neat little Jeep that he cruises around the forest roads in, enjoying a cup of coffee while checking on the scenery and wildlife. I assumed he wasn't going to come cruising by today. He's smarter than that. I think. But I could call him, hope that he was home, and ask him to fire up the Jeep for a rescue mission. A perfectly logical solution to a problem.

Except for one thing. Two years before this incident, I got stuck in almost the same spot under similar circumstances, at least with a different vehicle. Back then I had considered these same options and made the call to him. Marv had graciously dropped what he was doing, maybe pushed himself away from the supper table, and came to the rescue. I had thanked him profusely, offered him a drink back at the cabin, and promised not to be that stupid again.

So here I was again, stuck in a real hard place, literally and figuratively. Even though Marv was likely the best option, I was going to have to admit that nothing had been learned from the previous experience.

He still seemed like the best option. I gave Marv a call, got him to drop whatever important task he was involved in, and he and his Jeep again came to the rescue, winding their way down the snow-packed road. At least he knew where to find me. I just had to say—"same spot as two years ago." He and his little Jeep dragged my big tough truck back out onto the road without much effort. We had a good laugh and I once again promised to have learned a lesson. Hopefully he can forgive me for secretly wishing he'd get stuck once in a while, maybe just once, so I'd have a chance to rescue him.

There still might be a cost. Marv will probably talk about this incident to our mutual friends and neighbors. That may result in damage to my reputation as a savvy outdoorsman. Marv's wife Marie might even mention it to Marcie sometime in the future. I'll have to be prepared for that. But at least today I'd be home by supper time. I'm the cook in our family and Marcie likes to eat on time.

A Year in the Cabin Life

There are people who claim Minnesota has but two seasons—winter and road construction. Other Northlanders might throw in an extra or at least add "mosquito season" to the road construction. Still others, the purists I guess, would split the year into the four seasons of spring, summer, fall, and winter, clearly defined by months of the year. Then we have the real perfectionists. Those who go by dates driven by moon phases and ancient pagan rituals involving sacrifices, heavy drinking, and dancing around bonfires.

I personally think all these groups are taking a too-general look at our climate and seasonal social activities. For me, as a semi-retired cabin owner and outdoorsman, things get much more complicated. Seasons up here seem to be split by a messy week-by-week chronology. Let's have a look at these through my eyes in a less traditional fashion, and review them from the most disappointing "season" to the high point.

Let's start at "Late Summer." Late Summer is that period of time when the warm months are winding down, say from the second week of August to the end of Labor Day weekend. That's roughly a three or four week period where summer fun starts to come to an end. It includes late local festivals and the big finale of the State Fair, unless a virus or something like that gets in the way. For those of us who fish, warm water and hot days have cooled the bite. So it's time to face the music. The end is in sight.

Now comes an intense three weeks that I will term "Early Fall." If you are a cabin owner, lots of stuff has to happen. For me, it means dry docking and winterizing two or three or maybe even four boats depending on how well I've controlled my boat addiction. Just one will remain seaworthy for the upcoming duck hunting season. Dog Island, the floating swim raft, has to be paddled to shore and winched to its resting place. It's also time to take a serious look at the heating situation for the upcoming cold weather. Does the chimney need cleaning? Are there enough tarp-covered stacks of firewood drying out behind the outhouse? And, speaking of the outhouse, should I have it pumped out now to avoid a tragic situation in the cold frozen months ahead?

With this stuff done, we enter the start of about five weeks of "True Fall." About the last week of September, if you are trying to follow along that way. Night-time temperatures are dropping as fast as the sun, earlier and lower each day. The chipmunks, squirrels, and blue jays are all scrambling around competing for the last few acorns clanging down from the oak trees onto the pickup truck and the steel roof of the outhouse.

It's one of the bestest times of the year. Crimson maples, orange oaks, and bright gold aspen trees that hopefully hold onto their new colors for a few weeks of enjoyment. Grouse and woodcock are flushing ahead of Sage and Tikka down logging trails brilliantly lined with those colors. Flocks of ducks are wheeling over decoys spread off the islands. It's a fast five weeks that never seems to last long enough. Especially when there's a dock to deal with. Scheduling this chore is a delicate dance with Mother Nature. Why be a sheep blindly following the neighbors' examples and roll it to shore while weather and water are still warm? It might come in handy for one more duck hunt before the first skim-ice forms on some quiet October night or even into November for deer season.

Yes, that comes next. "Deer Season." This can last for almost six weeks if I am unlucky enough to not bag a deer early and thus lucky to stretch the season into early December. You will find me hunting deer the old-fashioned way, tip-toeing down the shores at dawn on the thin ice of a new season, wandering the lonely forest in a few inches of fresh snow, listening to the lakes alternating groaning in bass and pinging and ringing in soprano as ice musically forms. Maybe I will even find a deer.

Here comes the frenetic rush through the "Holiday Season." A final four weeks of the calendar year. It's a race to my fiscal year finish—selling books at holiday craft fairs, trying to get that one last event in. Another chance to connect with hardy Northlanders, talk about cabins and lakes, and take their money so I can dream about affording a kitchen and bathroom addition to the cabin. Time with family and friends. Cooking up a storm as the first blizzard rolls in. Planning the annual late December trip to the cabin. It will be cold, but if we aren't there, who's going to shoot the cannon off to ring in the New Year with an echoing blast out over the lake at midnight?

"Deep Winter" is finally here. A six-week period taking up January and a few weeks of February. Life goes into slow motion, almost freezing in time. It's a season for getting up late with the winter sun, having a couple cups of coffee, and thinking about what to do the rest of the day besides hauling firewood, stoking the stove, filling bird feeders, and watching the birds and squirrels empty the bird feeders. The sun will be setting on this short day once those important tasks are finished. Then, if the temperature is above ten below, and if the ATV starts, the evening bite might be starting out in the fish house.

If we make it through this cold hell, "Slow Winter" or "Dreaded Winter" arrives. Slow because the next four weeks seem to last forever, even longer than Deep Winter. Dreaded Winter because it's true Cabin Fever time. Doubts about your sanity arise, especially if efforts aren't made to get outside and do something. Which might still be hard since something like fourteen weeks of snow have built up in the forest and on the lake. The cabin's yard has shrunk, ringed with claustrophobic snow banks pushed high by Neighbor Bill's mighty Ford truck. It's a struggle to even get to the firewood stacks and keep a path to the outhouse clear. If there is a time to take a vacation to a warmer climate, this is it.

The good news is that by the middle of March, there is hope in "Early Spring." The days are longer, warmer, and visible changes are taking place. The south-facing slope below the cabin soaks up solar energy and melts open the trail down to the lake. You can hike or cross country ski to your heart's content, visiting islands and bays that haven't been seen for months, discovering what animals have survived, and what trees have succumbed to the weight of the winter. It's a whole new world to be explored before the ice pulls away from the shore and brings back memories of the sparkling clear water hidden below.

So now we have come to the middle of April. Hopefully "Spring" has sprung and it's time to get busy again. Time to get ready for the fishing opener in a handful of weeks. Three or four boats need to be retrieved from storage, de-winterized, and started—hopefully. There's always one that doesn't give up easy and requires multiple trips to town for batteries, fuel filters, spark plugs, and fresh gas. The lawn mower will demand some attention too. And let's not forget that the dock needs to be rolled in and adjusted, tackle boxes organized, gutters cleaned, and leaves raked. Time speeds up again, especially since it's also turkey hunting season and I'm getting up at four in the morning to watch the sunrise, commune with the flocks of newly arriving spring songbirds and maybe even one unlucky turkey.

One of my shortest seasons is now here. The two weeks between the opening day of fishing season and Memorial Day Weekend. We could call this "Late Spring" or maybe just cut to the chase and call it "Fishing Season."

The fish are biting! Take advantage of that situation, ease off on the cabin chores, and have some fun! I'm not much of a walleye fisherman. At least at the cabin. It's too much work and that's what God created Canada for. For me, there's nothing more relaxing than wandering down to the dock with a big cup of coffee and a couple of dogs, and leisurely trolling the shore of Crooked Lake for a northern pike, or two, or three. It's a guilty pleasure that sends me back down memory lane to mornings spent with my dad or Uncle Fred, sometimes on lakes just down the road from here.

It's worth mentioning that the Memorial Day holiday weekend is sometimes the best weekend of the year for cabin fun. The fish are on a feeding frenzy. The water might be warm enough for brave people to swim. The bugs around the campfire are manageable with enough smoke, bug repellent, S'mores, and adult beverages. The sun rises so early and the days last so long that the curtains on the cabin windows will be closed to allow sleeping in after a long night at the campfire. If the dogs let you.

Hang with me, folks! The end is near and the fun is just beginning. Let's call the next season "Early Summer"—the five weeks between Memorial Weekend and the Fourth of July. The pace of cabin life is picking up steam. The water should be, repeat should be, warm enough to swim without screaming. Dog Island is relaunched and invaded by swimmers and dogs and encircled by floaties. Maybe even a new fanciful pink unicorn will make a maiden voyage. Just try to ignore the gnats and mosquitoes that are mounting sneak attacks, while the deer flies circle your head in a full-on blitz and a wood tick or two crawls up a leg for a sure all-day case of the creepy-crawlies.

Finally, we are here! "High Summer." That five-week period between the Fourth of July and the end of the first weekend in August. Marcie coined this term when someone had the audacity to suggest an extended trip away from the cabin and lake. Time away from the lake when the floating is good, the fishing is above average, and the weather is tolerable. The bugs have abated. Local festivals are in full swing. Friends and family are hanging out at their places or stopping in for weekend visits. That says it all—it's family fun time at the lake.

Unfortunately there are those less self-aware who try to schedule self-important events during "High Summer." Class reunions in hot humid places where cornfields have replaced lakes. Weddings in small hot country churches where air conditioning is unheard of and the lake can be heard calling to you above the droning of the minister and the sobs of the bride. Conventions in southern cities where the rates are cheap —because there are no lakes and the heat—and lack of lakes—keeps well-paying customers away.

So listen up—it's High Summer. Most of us have lived forty-seven weeks waiting for this. Sit back and enjoy it with the rest of us. Don't be planning mandatory attendance events at this sacred time of the year. Weddings can wait. Babies can wait. If you absolutely have to schedule some important event, there had better be family, a lake, and a cabin involved.

The Wedding

The Wedding

Owning a lake cabin is a common dream for many Minnesotans and folks in other parts of the world. Hopefully a lot of them find the means to make this dream come true or at least find a way to squeeze in a vacation at one. It's a romantic scenario that some of us get to live, at least part-time. So let's take that romance up another notch or two—how about getting married at a lake cabin?

And so it came to pass that my oldest son Andy and his fiancé Stephanie, after many years of hanging around together and actual engagement, decided that our cabin would be the perfect "venue" (as they say in the wedding planning business) to tie the official knot.

Although I guess you could call it a "destination wedding," this wasn't going to be some heavily planned extravaganza. No white wedding tent pavilion. No catered sit-down eight-course meal. No hand-crafted arched arbor dripping with flowers in the background. The ceremony would be held down on the dock, at a time that weather permitted. Hundreds of people were not invited. In fact, Steph and Andy went down the same road Marcie and I did well over forty years ago. Only a few select friends and family were invited to attend.

Marcie and I approved of this concept. While we have enjoyed many big weddings for friends, family, and their offspring, we have never really felt the need. There were six people at our wedding—if you count the pastor and us. It worked, even if some close relatives feel slighted to this day. To each his or her own, and long may you live in happiness whatever your choice may be!

This plan sounded pretty simple and uncomplicated. But they did want to make it a memorable celebration and, as we found out, a low-impact, low-budget wedding doesn't actually make some things simpler when it's held at a rustic cabin. We weren't going to hire a caterer, tell them what to bring, and simply pay a bill for the food and the service. So there was menu planning, decisions about who was bringing what food and refreshment, and who was going to do the grilling. Because every cabin wedding I help plan needs a smoking grill with burning meat.

Next were the transportation and housing issues. Forget the usual limo trying to wind its way into the cabin on that narrow driveway. The bride decided that she and her entourage would arrive at the dock on a pontoon. This was a great idea given the limited space down at the dock. A pontoon would provide transportation to the ceremony, additional seating/standing room, and entertainment after the vows. How about a little cruise around the lake after the wedding ceremony? Wish I would have thought of that. But Marcie and I got married in February, if I remember right. It would have been hard to plan a pontoon ride in Minnesota then.

One problem was that while we owned the Big Boat, several fishing boats, a duck boat or two, a couple of canoes, four kayaks, a swim raft, and a bunch of floaties, we didn't own a pontoon. Luckily there are companies that rent and deliver those things. Problem solved except for the bill. They don't come cheap in July on Minnesota lake weekends.

Another complication should be evident to long-time members of my fan club. Our cabin lacks a formal bathroom. Those needs are taken care of by the quaint little outhouse tucked into the trees over by the firewood piles and boat trailers. It has worked out fine for our small family gatherings. But perhaps we could do better for a wedding with honored guests. Luckily there are rental companies to deal with this problem too. I made a couple of calls and soon had both a porta-toilet and hand sanitation station dialed in for delivery for the whole weekend.

Next came the real complicating factor. The Father-of-the-Groom usually has it pretty easy at weddings when compared to the other major players. He sits back, stays out of the way, takes orders, makes a short speech at the Groom's Dinner, and maybe pays a few bills. This should have been an even easier job for a small inexpensive wedding like this. It was not to be. Andy and Steph asked me to be the official for the ceremony.

Some people may cringe at the thought that a lay person, such as myself, can call themselves "Reverend" and legally perform weddings, funerals, and even baptisms via the magic of the internet. I understand. Don't do it then. I hadn't planned on this either until Andy and Steph made a simple and compelling argument for both the dock wedding and me as an official. "Why not do the wedding at a place we both know and love? And why not have it done by someone who knows and loves both of us?"

And so this too came to pass. I dutifully completed the internet paperwork, paid the fees, got my "How to Do a Wedding" instruction book complete with official forms, and filled out a few more forms and paid a few more fees with the local legal authorities. I also sought out professional advice from my own pastor who, by the way, was very supportive of this concept. I think he saw this as one less wedding he had to do, on a Saturday afternoon, in the summer, when he could be fishing.

Now I just had to start stressing out about what I was going to say. It had better be good, fit the setting, and be simple enough to be said with less than dry eyes. I cry easily after all—especially at weddings.

Luckily the rest of the planning came together without much of the drama that seems to be prevalent in wedding planning these days. When the day arrived, everything seemed to be in order. The guests arrived safely. The pontoon and portable toilet were delivered without a hitch. Nephew Brant agreed to be the pontoon chauffeur. Food and drink aplenty were packed into the fridge and coolers. I had a short ceremony planned including a few words of wisdom. Even the weather was predicted to be cooperative with sunny skies and eighty degrees.

Then things started to get complicated. I was sprucing up the front of the cabin shortly before the ceremony, tidying up the yard and arranging the recycling containers. Something started rustling around in the thick brush and trees on the hillside down to the lake. "Just another one of the herd of well-fed chipmunks and squirrels we support," I thought. Then I noticed a patch of black fur through an opening.

"Dammit, Sage," I yelled. "Get back here!" I know that was not very pastorly of me on this sacred day. But I had things to do and all four dogs were supposed to be shut in the cabin, not invited to the ceremony since the entire female side of the wedding party was wearing nice dresses. As informal as this affair was meant to be, they didn't want to get wet and permeated with dog stink should the Labradors decide to take a dock plunge during the service.

The black fur disappeared but Sage did not come romping up the hill. I yelled again and then headed down the lake trail to collect her. A big black furry creature did come out of the brush about ten feet from me. In this case it was one of our resident bears—not black Labrador Sage. I hastily backpedaled uphill yelling "BEAR!!!!" to warn the guests.

While the sound of my voice had not spooked the bear, seeing me at close quarters did. He headed the other way, crashing through the brush towards Neighbor Tom. My warning shout got Tom's attention. Safely on his deck, he looked down and called back—"Yup, that's what it is." Lucky for us the bear disappeared at a high rate of speed. He didn't return but did put everyone on edge. Our bears aren't very dangerous but they do like to eat. The thought of him or a relative showing up and ransacking the coolers or begging for brats from the grill was in the back of everyone's mind.

The next complication came while Andy and I and a few guests stood on the dock and awaited the arrival of the wedding pontoon. Minutes clicked away after the established time of arrival. The small group gathered on the dock anxiously looked at watches and cell phones. Had the pontoon died or hit a rock coming through Stony Point? Car trouble for the bride's party on the way to the public landing dock? Bridesmaid overboard? Questions mounted until the pontoon finally appeared across the lake, rounding the far point of Bird Island. It soon became clear what the problem was.

The fish were biting. What other wedding has had that problem? Steph had decided it was proper to fish in her wedding dress. Great Nephew Alex joined in while the others egged them on and cheered. The pontoon would glide ahead. Shouts of excitement would be heard. Brant would put it in neutral and coast to a stop while Steph or Alex wrestled in another northern pike. Then would come the laughter as the fish was swung aboard and forced to pose for pictures with the bride before being released. This occurred several times. Andy decided he might as well get in a few casts too. He grabbed a pole from the fishing boat and cast from the dock while the pontoon crept closer, fish by fish.

The pontoon finally reached the dock with all onboard laughing and chatting about the ride. We made room with the meager crowd split between the shore, the pontoon's spacious floor, and the dock. We even managed to get in a short wedding procession for the whole twenty feet of the dock with Allen, the bride's father, presenting her to Andy and me. Now the crunch was on. I had to perform and do so with wet eyes.

So I got down to business. Every wedding should have that movie-moment where the pastor asks if anyone objects to this union. The audience members look around, not really expecting anyone to come forth, but perhaps secretly hoping for a little drama. In this case, I tried to cut that off. I brought eleven-year-old Bailey to the front. She was about to become The Granddaughter should she approve. "Bailey—you are the only other person who has a say in this. Do you approve of Andy and Steph getting married?" She usually isn't at a loss for words with me. In this case she just nodded her head and ducked back to the safety of the wedding party.

After that and a few introductory remarks, I felt compelled to give a short sermon. One I felt was appropriate for the setting and the occasion. At least I tried to say these things. But like I said before, I cry easily at weddings. I might have stumbled, mumbled, and forgot a few of these.

"As a father and an old guy, I'm full of advice. So this sermon is my chance to officially give some. I won't call it free advice—because you, Andy, have cost me a lot. And not just money. But I've got much back. Fun watching you play baseball games. Companionship on hunting and fishing trips. Things like that.

Steph, I'm grateful for what you have brought us. Two more family members to share life with, among many other things.

Cabin Fever

I'm glad you both chose this place, the cabin, the lake, the forest, and the dock. They are all places we know and love. And, when you think about it, this place is a lot like a relationship and a marriage will be for you guys.

I always knew I wanted a piece of land, a cabin to call mine, a lake to fish and learn about. Land to hike and hunt. Andy, Steph—I'm sure it's like looking for a girlfriend, a boyfriend, a partner in life—a wife or a husband. You know you want someone that you can make memories with, grow with, have fun with, and go through life's trials and tribulations with.

So there's that—something you always wanted. But now here comes the advice. This place, the cabin, the land, the dock—none of them are perfect and never will be. Just like most relationships.

The hill here is a tough climb up to the cabin. It takes some effort to enjoy.

The cabin is small and rustic. But it still takes time and effort to maintain.

There's nasty bugs that live here in the forest. And poison ivy. The fish don't always bite in the lake and there's no walleyes out there that we know of. It could be better. It ain't perfect.

And we all know about the outhouse! That's inconvenient and takes some effort to use in the dark of the night or the dead of winter.

But look at the view from up top in the fall—or from down here on the dock once you have pushed past the inconvenience and made an effort to get here. Or how nice and dry the cabin is in a rain storm or warm and cozy in the winter. Or how much fun it is to fish when the crappies are biting. Even the outhouse has some advantages.

So expect to put effort into your relationship. Just like this place, it won't be perfect. Expect inconveniences. There will be highs and lows, some of which I know you have already experienced.

That may be sobering. But think about the good news.

We are here on the dock, with family, with friends, on this lovely day. Let's put some effort into making it a day to remember."

With that we moved to the vows and then the exchange of rings, which went well and did not involve someone swimming in wedding clothes for an overboard ring. The rest of the day went smoothly too. The victory lap around the lake on the pontoon. The grilling of the brats and burgers. No bear wedding crashers. A few good neighbors, friends, and relatives to share the moment with. Finally, a beautiful late afternoon and evening spent cruising the lake on the pontoon.

So how's that? A wedding at the cabin on the lake. Pretty damn romantic. I know there are those out there who might also be saying—"Yeah—and pretty dang cheap too." Yes—it was. Except for one thing. We all enjoyed that pontoon. We enjoyed it so much that we bought one. That added to the final cost.

Maybe I can use my experience and lower the bill by performing lake and cabin weddings for others. After all, I now have both an official license and a pontoon.

Cabin Fever

Interested? Give a call for your cabin and dock wedding plans. I might be able to work you into the schedule if the fish aren't biting. Just be aware that I work cheap, but the pontoon rental is gonna cost you . . .

A Kayak-Kinda Night

A Kayak-Kinda Night

There are nights, when the family is hanging around the cabin, when we board whoever is willing onto Ruby the Pontoon and idle away from the dock. We probably don't fish, just take a leisurely cruise looking for loon chicks, deer fawns, otters, and other wildlife and cabin lovers enjoying the tranquil lake with us. There are other nights when the family isn't around and Marcie decides to read on the deck. On these nights I might load the dogs and fishing gear into the little boat and troll laps. The dogs perch on the bow deck, alert for wildlife, while I trail a fishing lure behind and enjoy a beverage. I might even stop along the way for quiet conversation with neighbors doing the same thing. But some nights are kayak-kinda nights. Rare nights where I'm alone with no other responsibilities or hangers-on and the lake is empty of other boats. Just me, the lake, and a kayak.

This is one of those nights. Clad in swimming suit and water shoes, I wade into the warm water, load a couple of fishing rods into rod holders, and slide into the tan fishing kayak for an evening paddle. I'm taking a risk on the weather. The smartphone zipped into a water-proof plastic bag has warned that the threatening sky to the west will bring wind, rain, and thunder in a couple hours, right before dark. Hopefully the electronic weatherman is right. It's worth a chance.

The paddle across the channel to Big Island works

the glitches out of my arms, stretches the back, and encourages me to pick up speed to not waste precious kayak-time. I take a hard right down the channel between the island and the main shore, pushing aside lily pads the size of Thanksgiving Day meat platters, sending minnows and small fish scattering ahead, rippling the still water.

The channel narrows to stream-width where two big rocks lurk below the surface, smeared with the silver scrapings of aluminum fishing boats that tried to navigate through and left their marks. At the narrowest part, tall cattails close in on both sides. Beavers, otters, deer, and other critters use this spot as a crossing, beating down a muddy narrow path through the weedy jungle to the water. Here is where daughter-in-law Steph claims a spooked deer jumped right over the kayak while she was paddling through, alone on a kayak-kinda night. I believe her—sort of. After all she's a fisherperson and prone to stretch the truth like the rest of us.

Up ahead through the window of the narrows, is the kayak-kinda place I'm headed to on this kayak-kinda night. A small bay surrounded by high, forested hillsides. The main lake is rarely busy. This pristine little bay gets even fewer visitors. Only one dock is visible. The boat that goes with it is pulled on shore with the motor tilted, propeller in the air. Looks like I'll be the only person marring the view tonight.

A young wood duck skitters across the surface, too young to fly, flapping wings lapping the water as it screeches and heads for the sanctuary of the tall weeds on the north side. On the other shore, the red coat of a whitetail doe stands out, her reflection mirroring on the water as she wades knee-deep, nosing in the shallows for tasty weeds. I expect to see a fawn behind her and slowly glide the kayak that way. Barely dipping the paddle in the water, while trying to stealthily remove the phone with its camera out of the waterproof bag. How close can I get? She's aware of my intrusion, flicking her tail and glancing my way while continuing to forage. At fifty yards she gives me a watery stomping splash with a front hoof and bounds up the bank, huffing and snorting as she goes.

My concentration on the doe allows another bay resident to sneak close to the kayak. A beaver slaps his tail on the water behind me, the echoing smack almost causing me to drop that expensive smartphone into the wet bottom of the kayak. I spin around to face him. I thought the old decrepit beaver hut wasting away on the shore was uninhabited. I guess not. Another beaver head pops up near it and glides through the water, patrolling back and forth in front of the stick-covered home while the first one hangs in the middle of the bay, eyes barely above the water, repeatedly slapping that wide flat tail to decoy me away. Back onshore, the doe keeps snorting from the forest, also highly offended by the disturbance in her bay.

They've all been distractions from the weather. A loon calling overhead on a fly-by brings my attention to the dark clouds building in the western sky. It looks like that smartphone weatherman was overly optimistic about those two hours. It's not going to be a kayak-kinda night much longer.

I leave the wildlife to the privacy of their paradise and start stroking hard for the channel, the only way out. I'm powering through, concentrating on missing the rocks, when a snort and movement to the left scares me again. Standing in the crossing, a paddle's length away, is a fork-horn buck, antlers still fuzzy with velvet. He's knee-deep in the mud, no doubt trying to decide if he can jump my kayak like he or a relative did Steph's. Once again I fumble for the phone camera.

The buck teases me. Lets me get the phone out of the dry bag. Then he spins and bounds back into the forest, waving his fluffy white tail in retreat before my wet finger print can activate the phone and power up the camera. There's no time to curse my luck at missing an award-winning photo. The wind gusts down the channel from the little bay, pushing the kayak forward as a warning of the coming storm.

I'm in trouble now. I must paddle hard down the protected island shore and then venture out across the channel to the dock—not a kayak-kinda place with the west winds of the storm front howling and concentrated in the wind tunnel between the island and the shore. I brave the channel and power on towards the dock, through wind and waves, spray soaking my meager clothing to the skin. I try not to think of the metal paddle blade flashing furiously in my hands or the unused fishing poles poking high in the air behind. I paddle harder, trying to be a challenging moving target for the weather gods chucking lightning bolts my way.

I slide up to the dock as lily pads begin to ripple

and flap in the gusts and the first huge rain drops splatter. I jump into the water, shove the kayak up on shore, toss the paddle off to the side and escape the lake, stride up the hill as fast as these old legs will take me. Hopefully the old aspen trees lining the path will hold in the winds of one more storm and not come crashing down just yet. It looks like it's time for a cabin-kinda night in a sheltered cabin-kinda place.

The Big Switch

I've never tried to write real complicated stuff. I actually promote my books, and myself, as "This ain't *War and Peace* and I'm not Tolstoy either." Some people get it, even other writers. One professional reviewer of my first book stated that she loved *Firewood Happens* "because of its lack of deep thoughts." Some writers might have been insulted. But I had to say, "Yup, that's me." Forget all of that for a moment and try to pay attention in the following story. It's kinda complicated and maybe confusing. After all, the subject is my current boat inventory.

Let's get the easy stuff out of the way first. My current inventory (including Marcie's share) includes four non-motorized kayaks, two canoes, and a paddle boat. But wait, I already forgot The Granddaughter's little mini-kayak. I guess that is technically gifted to her but it's in my possession so maybe I should include that. So that's seven —or eight—uncomplicated, un-motorized watercraft depending on how you count them.

I also know where they all are, so this part of the inventory is easy. At least I think I do. The last time I saw the old aluminum canoe, it was lying alongside son Andy's garage. It's probably still there. Not included in this list is the floating swim raft, AKA "Dog Island." Let's not get further confused in trying to decide if that's a "watercraft" even though it is officially registered with the local authorities.

Things get a little more complicated when trying to round up the potentially motorized watercraft. There's two small 14-foot aluminum duck/fishing boats still floating around. I know one of them is wasting away on the old boat winch back in the weeds on the east side of the dock. The other one might be on a duck hunting lake south of our hometown. At least that's where son Steve and his friends parked it over ten years ago. Maybe that's where those missing duck decoys are too. I might have to brave the swamp some day and check.

Now on to the bigger boats. Until just recently, the motorized inventory of boats was pretty simple. Then things got complicated. So try to follow along here. First there's "The Big Boat," a 1987 Fish-and-Ski model that I picked up at a boat show in 1989. Let's not worry about "The Big Boat" any more. It's safely parked in the garage, worked fine on the family camping trip to Ely and need not be discussed again in the context of this story. If you're paying attention, we are now up to eight or nine depending on if you include The Granddaughter's kayak. Maybe we should just include it and call it number nine. So I will.

Next is the old 14-foot Lund fishing boat that was offered to me for a criminally low price from a friend of a relative when that guy needed to buy his teenager a car. Bad for him, good for me. That's a trade I would have agonized over but do understand. I once had to trade a fishing boat for a clothes dryer back in the day when the first baby showed up. Sometimes things just happen. I graciously let Marcie have her way with that decision. Let's call the Lund number ten in our ongoing inventory.

The Lund came with a 25-horse motor that served us well for several years. It got Andy and me into and out of the wilderness of northern Minnesota on a moose hunt. It was a tough, adventurous trip that resulted in a leaking crack in the boat's hull from being overloaded with moose hunting gear. Luckily the motor kept running and got us back to civilization unharmed. At least until it died, with a clunk and a cloud of smoke, on the opening day of fishing season a few years later. I happened to have an old 6-horse motor lying around. The boat continued on severely underpowered. Here's where big changes started to happen.

Marcie has complained about that Lund for years. It doesn't have a flat floor or comfortable seats and can get a little small with her and me and two dogs trying to fish. I attempted several upgrades to appease her. Like padded swivel seats and raised plywood decks for the dogs to sit on. But the lack of a floor still was a problem and it took forever to get to a fishing spot on the other side of the lake with the little 6-horse motor groaning away, her complaining, and the dogs balancing on their little doggie decks.

Maybe more power would help. At least Marcie would have more time fishing and maybe less time complaining. So I tracked down a nearly new 20-horse motor with quiet, modern, 4-stroke technology. I managed to fit the motor to the Lund despite the fact it was a long shaft motor and the boat's transom was made for a short shaft. They sell adapter kits for problems like that. The result was better in some ways. We got to fishing spots quicker. But I could still hear complaints about comfort. In fact, I could hear them loud and clear since this new motor was so quiet you could hear complaints even at full speed.

It was time for drastic action. Technically all I needed was to replace the boat since the motor and trailer were fine. I started surfing internet market places looking for a bigger, more comfortable, non-leaking orphan boat that needed a new motor and a new home.

Orphan boats aren't as common as I thought they would be. Maybe since this is Minnesota and us hearty outdoorsy residents like boats to use on the 11,842 lakes the DNR counts. Eventually one did show up that looked too good to pass up. By now it was October and the boat market had become a buyers' market since nobody was going to be using one for another seven or eight months. The current owner professed that he wanted to get rid of a surplus boat rather than paying to store it. That seemed like a pretty slim excuse to get rid of a boat and it was a complete boat, motor, trailer combo when all I really needed was a boat. But maybe I could sell the unneeded motor and trailer next spring and make some money. Maybe ...

Marcie and I drove an hour or so to another town and looked the situation over. The trailer wasn't much. However, the boat and motor looked good and Marcie got to sit in the boat and pronounce it big enough and comfortable enough for her and the dogs. I got her to promise to quit complaining, we handed over some money, and pulled away with boat number eleven if you are keeping up. That seems like quite a few, but at least we were confident that our boat needs were satisfied for the foreseeable future.

That feeling of confidence lasted all of a couple of months. In my defense, I didn't go looking for any more boats or any more boat problems. Sometimes they just seem to find me, maybe because of my reputation for having many boats and wanting more. In this case, Marcie and I had mentioned to some friends how much the family enjoyed the pontoon that was rented for Andy and Steph's wedding. One of those friends called me in the dead of winter with a proposition.

"Mike," Bill said, "Bonnie and I have decided to sell our pontoon and get a new one. This one isn't big enough for the kids, grandkids, friends, and dogs, and they all claim it doesn't go fast enough. The dealer doesn't like to take trades. Would you be interested?" He proceeded to name a very attractive price.

I think you know where this part of the story is going. Not only was I unable to resist, Marcie thought it was a good idea. Both of us had been on this actual pontoon and liked it. The kids also thought it was a good idea and offered to help out with the cost. That was a first and sure sign to me that they may have inherited some of the family affection for boats. It also helped that we were in the beginning phases of a pandemic and the thought of social distancing on the lake on a spacious pontoon was even more inviting.

So we made the deal. Of course we did. It even came with a name and a reputation as a serious party and fishing barge. I pulled "Ruby" and her spacious seats, pop-up privacy room, live well for the fish, and big 4-stroke motor to her new home at the cabin.

There you might think is the end of this story. We are up to twelve "things that float." Surely that is enough for any man, woman, or family, even as a cabin owner in Minnesota. In this case you are right. In fact, I decided to reverse this trend. Registration and repair fees were adding up. Storage space in my friend's shed was maxed out, especially when you consider Marcie's camper trailer was parked there too. We also needed room around the cabin yard to park cars and campers when the kids showed up with their families and dogs. Something had to go.

The obvious contender in my mind was the Lund fishing boat. It was sitting derelict and unused over by the outhouse, gathering leaves and mouse nests and growing plants in its transom from the compost. Still, it wasn't an easy decision. It had the best motor and trailer. So hold on, bear with me, and try to follow along.

I relayed both the Lund and the new fishing boat down to the lake access with a little help from nephew Brant. (Remember his name. It comes up later.) There we floated the boats off their current trailers. Wait—I forgot to mention we also pulled another boat trailer down there too. One that had been sitting back in the woods unused for "a few years." We loaded the new boat onto the Lund's now former trailer, and removed the motor it came with. Next we loaded the Lund onto the trailer from the woods and removed the almost new 20-horse motor from it.

The motor from the new boat went into the back of the pickup. The Lund's 20-horse went onto the new boat. While we were at it, we pulled that old fishing boat, mentioned at the beginning of the story, out of the weeds down by the dock, and put it on the crappy trailer the new boat came on. This got hauled back to the cabin and stuck in the woods where the Lund's new trailer once was.

If you followed all that, I ended up with the new boat on the Lund's trailer with the Lund's motor. The Lund was sitting on a formerly abandoned trailer without a motor. And the new boat's former trailer was parked in the woods with a formerly abandoned boat on it. And the new boat's former motor was in the back of the pickup.

Big deal, you might say. There's still too many boats and now there's a couple without motors. Here's where I finally made progress on my inventory reduction project. The motor from the new boat went up for sale on an internet market place and was snatched up at a good price (for me anyway) by a guy who needed a motor to keep his kid happy while duck hunting. The old abandoned boat and the crappy trailer went to their final resting place at a junk yard, hopefully to be recycled and reincarnated into new boats and trailers. So we were down to eleven boats by now. I think.

Next came the Lund. I considered putting that old 6-horse back on it and selling it. That plan seemed problematic. The trailer was old, rusty, and equipped with rotting tires from sitting back in the woods for double-digit years. The boat still had the leaking crack in the hull from our moose hunt that needed to be patched several times a year if you wanted dry feet while fishing. And the 6-horse motor had seen better days and only ran when the weather was hot and it felt like it. Then I had an epiphany.

Brant, the nephew mentioned before who helped with the big switch, has a thirteen-year-old son who loves fishing. He didn't have a boat. What better way to teach a youngster the joys of boat ownership than to graciously donate him an old boat with a rusty trailer, rotting tires, and a leaking hull? I even threw in an old electric motor just because I was feeling good about the deal. I almost included the old 6-horse motor too. I had second thoughts after remembering all the bad words I had called it over the last few years. Perhaps he wasn't ready for that much boat ownership joy or learning those bad words, just yet.

I suppose I could end this with a test and see how many readers can email me with the correct boat inventory. I could even offer up a free book or two as a prize. But to tell you the truth, I'm a little confused myself. And these things seem to change quite often.

Fear of Fly-Fishing

Fear of Fly-Fishing

A recent social media post from one of my favorite conservation organizations profiled an appointee to a major Federal Government Cabinet Post. The piece included a picture of the guy (a self-submitted publicity shot, I assume), standing in the middle of a picturesque mountain stream, fly-fishing in mid-cast. Given my interest in this agency's work, I read the whole piece and even dove into the "Comments" sections. We all know how dangerous that can be. Right or wrong, true or false, the comments mainly tore this guy up and expressed severe reservations about his suitability for this role. They even went so far as to criticize his fly-casting skills based on that one photo.

"Wooo-eeee," I thought. "This is a tough crowd. I wonder what they would say if they saw me trying to fly-fish in Yellowstone National Park?"

After over sixty years of fishing, I can claim proficiency (should that be pro_fish_iency?) with almost any type of fishing equipment. Gill nets, trawls, cast nets, seines, spears, downriggers, tip-ups, bait casters, open-face spinners, Zebco 202s—I've used them all and used them well. Except for a fly-rod . . .

This glaring experience gap became evident a few years ago when Marcie and I planned our first empty-nester road trip out West. After a stop in South Dakota's Black Hills for a family campout, we planned an itinerary that included legendary fly-fishing destinations like Yellowstone National Park and the Gallatin National Forest. Now, I do own a fly-rod and some of the related equipment. However, I have to admit it was purchased in the 1980s for about two dollars at a hardware store sidewalk sale and hasn't been used much since.

"No problem," I thought. "I'll just pick up some flies on the way west, get in some practice at the Black Hills, and be ready when we hit those famed Rocky Mountain rivers."

I did manage to get some fancy-looking dry flies and a few bead-headed nymphs at a sports shop in South Dakota. My attempts to practice with them failed when other responsibilities took priority. The lake at the campground was full of rainbow trout, common targets for fly-fishermen. But they were wary and sulking in deep water to avoid the summer heat and boat traffic. They weren't willing to rise to the near surface to examine fake flies presented by an amateur. So I did something that means a true fly-fisherman will never vote for me in a political election or support my nomination to an important post, should either unlikely circumstance happen. I broke out the Minnesota-style crappie/walleye fishing tackle and started catching them on bait.

My success was noted by two young non-fishing nephews from Colorado. They asked for instructions. Once again, I'd ask those dedicated fly-fisher types not to be too judgmental. I wouldn't take a first-time fisherman out muskie fishing in Minnesota. Muskies are often referred to as "The Fish of 10,000 Casts." Casting 9,999 times without a bite is not a good experience for first-timers. So I didn't push fly-tackle, complicated casting techniques, and my limited skills off on these young rookies. I set them up with night crawlers and spinning tackle, fishing on the bottom in twenty feet of still lake water. Kinda like fishing for bullheads in a green southern Minnesota lake. One of them hooked a big 16-inch rainbow almost immediately and succeeded in wrestling it near shore. His brother splashed in knee-deep with his clothes on to help land it. Most of my fishing time over the next five days was "wasted" hanging out with these guys and having a blast while doing it.

With the family campout behind us, Marcie and I headed farther west with the truck packed with gear and two kayaks strapped to the roof. We wound our way into the east side of Yellowstone National Park and cruised down the Lamar River Valley, headed for our lodging in the central part of the park.

The Lamar River looked like a great place to try out my fly-fishing equipment. Other guys apparently thought the same and were to be seen standing mid-river, gracefully floating fly-line out behind them and then moving it forward to gently lay a fake bug on the surface of the river. I used the term "to be seen" in that sentence on purpose. Forget about my basic equipment and skills for one moment. It was obvious that I was severely underdressed for the occasion.

I have never thought of fishing as being a sport of the fashion-conscious. I planned on wading the river dressed in my usual fishing uniform of camo jeans, a pair of wet shoes, a T-shirt and a Minnesota Twins baseball hat. That was not going to cut it here, on the famed waters of the West, where well-dressed, apparently rich, and maybe famous anglers come to strut the river bank runways like New York fashion models.

Let's start with the footwear. Every one of these guys (and they were mostly guys) were sporting gray or khaki waders. No tennis shoes. No Minnesota boat/beach shoes. No camo neoprene waders like the ones I left back home. The waders were protecting high quality fishing pants of light-weight fabric of a matching color. Their shirts might be a slightly different shade of gray or khaki, just for a bit of fashion contrast but always had button-down collars and half-rolled-up sleeves. I saw none wearing camo jeans.

Next was the vest. I do own a down vest to keep me warm. A grouse hunting vest with patches of orange to keep me safe and visible in the grouse thickets. A turkey hunting vest with big pockets for turkey calls and a built-in seat cushion. I do not own a fly-fishing vest. I figured a plastic container of flies stuffed in a jeans pocket would be good enough. Nope. Every one of these fashionable anglers was sporting what appeared to be the same light gray fishing vest with many pockets for equipment and little patches of fluffy fake sheepskin to dry their flies on. Hat? Same thing. Whoever patented wide-brimmed, mesh-sided, light gray hats must be making a fortune.

It's time here to admit that I am vulnerable to

social pressure. It's part of the whole Minnesota Scandinavian thing after all. It's not in our DNA to be the one standing out in a crowd. In this case, that would have been me, wading the river looking like some guy who decided to drive out from Minnesota and try fishing in his cabin clothes with a Coast-To-Coast hardware store fly-rod. So those fly-fishing plans got changed. I'd have to find a quiet spot where practice in my hillbilly fishing outfit could go unobserved.

Ever try to find a quiet unobserved spot in Yellowstone National Park in the middle of the summer tourist season? That's not going to happen, unless you are willing to pack a couple cans of bear spray and take a hike into the backcountry, preferably with someone you don't love and can outrun in the event of a hungry and/or angry grizzly bear encounter. Since Marcie didn't fit that description and wasn't too keen on the whole grizzly-bear-encounter thing, I put my fishing plans on hold.

It's a good thing there's plenty to do at Yellowstone. We thoroughly enjoyed our stay, saw all the major sights, and found a new hobby. Much time was spent at wildlife overlooks, meeting new friends from all over the world, while watching buffalo, elk, and the occasional wolf interact, oblivious to all the eyes watching them from afar. Note to all those Park Rangers and Ranger Rick Wannabees out there—sorry (sort of), they will always be buffalo, not bison, to me.

I did miss fishing, especially with all this prime-looking water around. I will also admit to being at least a little bit jealous of one guy we spotted fishing the

Madison River on the western edge of the park. He stood waist-deep in the river, a guy about my age, flawlessly moving his assumed very expensive fly-rod back and forth, effortlessly laying out casts in his high fashion outfit, the sun sparkling off the river water and shining on the mountains behind him. A pair of snow-white trumpeter swans drifted in the river, an arm's length away, just to add a little extra ambiance.

This was all good but what really topped off the scene was the truck parked alongside the river in the foreground. An early-1960s Chevy, like the ones I grew up riding around farm country in. The engine and other mechanical equipment must have been rebuilt since it bore license plates from Indiana and must have successfully made the road trip here. The body still looked like something you'd find on a Midwest farm—patches of rust here and there and a mismatched-color driver's side door. I'll remember that mental picture for a long time, like the painting on the cover of some highbrow fly-fishing magazine. I wanted to be that guy.

I was tempted to update my fishing wardrobe once we hit civilization in the booming tourist town of West Yellowstone. However, while standing in line at a fast food joint, I noticed that a mediocre burger was going to cost me about three times what it would back home. Two all-beef patties with pickles and special sauce on a sesame seed bun weren't needed that bad. We got a decent burger at a local spot for about the same price and headed north out of town without checking the prices of fishing gear in this Disneyland tourist trap.

Fear of Fly-Fishing

Next on the agenda was a secluded cabin deep in the mountains of the Gallatin National Forest, conveniently located on a trout stream. It was here that the chance might come to try out that primitive fly-fishing gear packed unused in the back of the truck. We wound our way back into the mountains, thanking the truck's four-wheel drive several times, and eventually found the rental cabin. It was located at the end of the road near a backpacking trail headed off into the mountains looming above. But guess what? Standing in the river, at the trail parking lot, was a guide, loudly giving a client fisherman instructions on how to fly-fish. He also appeared to provide fashion guidance along with casting instructions. They were identically dressed in the light gray waders, pants, shirt, vest, and hat uniform I had seen all through Yellowstone National Park.

Luckily our cabin was located on a short side road and provided us privacy from the parking area and distance from these dudes. We got settled into the cabin, built a campfire outside, and pulled up our chairs for a quiet evening. Deer wandered by unafraid while the fire crackled and the stream babbled past our toes. This could be paradise if the fish would cooperate in the morning.

The morning dawned bright and sunny with a heavy dew and chill mountain air. I set off upriver from the cabin and parking lot. The deeper I got into the bush, the less chance I was going to have to deal with some dude fisherman and critiques of my equipment, technique, and wardrobe. I crashed off into the willow- and brush-choked river bottom, getting off the beaten path and into the difficult spots where dudes fear to tread lest they rip their gold-plated waders and sweat-stain the pits of their fancy shirts.

There I found trout-fishing paradise in the form of beaver ponds staggered along the stream with clear Rocky Mountain water flowing over them and spilling around the twisting and turning rocky stream banks. It was the stuff beer commercials are made from.

It looked like perfect grizzly bear country too. Which added something to the atmosphere given that I was not packing bear spray or a gun or fishing with a slow-running companion. I relied on making plenty of noise, trying to sound like a larger, meaner, profane bear as I stumbled through the brush and willows, tripping over beaver logs, fighting in towards the river bank. It worked. I didn't find any bears. I did find trout.

I flipped a small white Minnesota crappie jig into the stream flow with my short little Minnesota crappie spinning rod. Yes, I had gone over to the dark side; at least that's what rabid fly-fishermen would say. Too bad. I always say, "If you can't join them, find a way to beat them!"

It was time to have some fun and forget about dude fishermen. Besides, who wants to try to drag a ten-foot long fly-rod through the brush and then try to figure out how to cast in the confines of a tree- and brush-choked stream? A bit of silver flashed away from a rock in the clear water and attacked the jig. I wrestled a 10-inch brook trout to the bank, flipped it out of the water like a dock sunfish, and pounced on it in the gravel of the river bank. Brook trout are one of Mother Nature's most colorful handiworks, masterpieces of art that swim. Spotted brownish-green tops and sides, scarlet bellies, and contrasting cream-white fin tips. I admired this first trout and took in what I call a "Western Moment." A beautiful fish, with mountains towering in the background, as the stream coursed past my feet. It would have made a nice picture to go with the story, except some guy would have taken umbrage to my wardrobe of wet hiking shoes, camo jeans, sweat shirt, and a baseball hat, and my choice of fishing equipment. So let's keep that image to ourselves.

Some might also take exception to what happened next. I thumped the fish on the head, strung it up on a make-shift willow branch stringer, and went looking for more. That's one of the beauties of catching brook trout in western streams. While they might be worshipped back in the Midwest, here they are an invasive species, crowding out native trout like the famed cutthroat and bull trout. The fishing regulation authorities encourage you to turn them into tasty meals instead of releasing them to fight with the local trout. They are tasty—like miniature salmon.

I brought a few back to the cabin and we had breakfast of crisped-up trout in bacon grease in a cast iron frypan over a campfire. I repeated the fishing excursion later in the afternoon and procured more. That night we had our own private wine and fire-roasted brook trout party in paradise, watching the sun sink into the mountains and listening to the brook babbling past our chairs.

We headed back east toward home the next morning. The long drive across monotonous prairies gave us plenty of time to plan the next trip. I'll probably work on my fly-fishing technique back home and maybe even pick up a hat and vest. That might give me the courage to step out into one of the more public trout streams and risk a fashion critique. But it is unlikely that anyone is ever going to see me and be jealous of "that dude fisherman from Minnesota."

The Compleat Coffee Drinker

One of the simple joys of cabin life is to take that first cup of morning coffee out onto the deck and plop down in an easy chair in the morning sun to watch the dogs play, the hummingbirds hum, and the chipmunks do silly chipmunk things. I've tried it without coffee on those few but terrible mornings when the cabin's coffee stash is gone and SOMEBODY forgot to add it to the grocery list. It's just not the same. Drinking coffee adds a justifiable purpose to the activity besides that morning jolt of caffeine.

Sipping coffee on the deck is one of the easiest tasks a coffee drinker faces. You got your easy chair. You got your no-spill sippy cup just in case a dog tail knocks it off the railing. You just need to call back into the cabin to let your Significant Other know that a refill is needed. It becomes much more difficult when trying to enjoy coffee while participating in outdoor sports.

Take coffee drinking while fishing as an example. There's nothing like a few laps around the lake in the morning, trolling for northern pike while drinking coffee. It's one of those simple pleasures in life. The boat also has a nice comfortable seat and cup holders for sippy cups. This is important. Coffee is a much more precious commodity out in the boat since refills may be back at the cabin and the Significant Other may be in the boat with you or may not be willing to truck a refill down to the dock. Especially if that Significant Other decided to sleep in while you and the dogs fish. You have also added a complicating activity. A fish may hit while taking a long sip, causing you to try to get the cup back in the holder with one hand, steer the boat with another, and grab the fishing rod with the third.

But you ain't seen nothing yet. I'm also a hunter. A coffee-drinking hunter. Hunting usually takes place during some of the colder months of the year. That first cup of coffee in the duck blind or deer stand has now become a necessity, a matter of survival, a way to keep the insides warm while waiting for the day's quarry to show up. If it's duck season, there may be a cold wet hunting dog trying to snuggle up to you. If it's deer season, the deer stand high in the trees may be swaying in the breeze and have limited room. In both cases, there's also a loaded gun to worry about. Things have gotten complicated. So let's look at how to deal with these factors via experience and technology.

First, a word about coffee selection. You may like the weak church-lady coffee you grew up with. The stuff that comes pre-ground in three pound cans. That's fine— for you. I'm going with something darker, thicker, and stronger—something that will hold up to the rigors of being touted around in a storage device most of the day. It doesn't have to be the whole bean grind-as-you-go stuff or even the top-shelf latest trend from a small obscure island where the monkeys have to eat it first. It does have to be dark roast and cheap enough that I don't have to wrestle with my inner Scandinavian. I'm going to use a lot of it. In case you are wondering, I don't feel that caffeine-free selections need be mentioned here.

I'm also okay with the use of a good old-fashioned electric drip coffee maker instead of a French press or some other highbrow brewer. The electric brewer has a timer and does double-duty as an alarm clock. In our small cabin, the gurgle of the brewer and the smell of fresh coffee is usually enough to get me out of the sack. If it doesn't, the dogs know the routine and will give me the cold nose treatment to get up and fill their breakfast bowls.

Now let's talk about capacity. I really hate to resort to the use of an old, tired cliché, but in this case, it does say it all. "Size does matter." It matters in the size of the brewer, the cup, and the storage device we will discuss at length shortly. The brewer has to make enough coffee for your needs, possibly that of the Significant Other, and any other coffee-drinking freeloaders who happen to be hanging around. Those trendy single-cup brewers aren't gonna cut it.

The size of the brewer has to take into account cup size, how much will be drunk off-site in the fishing boat, duck blind, or deer stand, and it must factor in the spillage factor. Ever missed your cup while pouring? Ever had a dog tail knock a freshly poured non-spill-proof cup over? Ever just plain missed your mouth and hit your beard and clothes instead? If you haven't, you aren't me. You need to consider history and take this fact of life into account to be a compleat coffee drinker.

Cup size is perhaps the least important factor in

the whole spillage equation. Carrying a spare cup out into the Great Outdoors is both clumsy and inefficient. And in extremely cold weather, whatever the size, it's going to get cold quick. I usually just stick with whatever size cup comes screwed to the top of the storage container. These are not spill-proof but they are handy and portable. Just make sure you have it. Drinking straight from the storage container is possible but not recommended. Especially if you are sharing.

So let's talk about coffee storage devices now. These are arguably the most important part of the capacity question and formula. I realize that "coffee storage device" is a clumsy term. But trust me, using it is easier than figuring out how to put a trademark symbol above a certain trademarked name every time I'm tempted to use it. There are some things they don't teach in the DIY writers' classes I've taken. So let's abbreviate it and coin a new term—"CSD."

When choosing a CSD, many factors must be taken into consideration. Capacity is hugely important. So is the construction material and the pouring technology. Color does not matter. I repeat—color does not matter! This may seem strange if you picture me in total camouflage clothing, sitting in a camouflage duck blind with a dog wearing a camouflage neoprene vest, waving a bright pink or red CSD around. Trust me on this for now. We will discuss it later.

So in the CSD selection process, I recommend going to a large store with an ample selection. Forget the internet sites. You want to handle these in person. First rule out all the CSDs that are constructed with plastic exteriors and glass inserts. The plastic is going to crack the first time the dog knocks it off the boat seat or when it slips from your cold gloved hand in the deer stand. When you pick it up, there will be a tinkling sound coming from within, sort of like ices cubes in a cold drink. That's not ice cubes you're hearing. It's the broken shards of the glass insert that shattered in the fall. Unless you like a little pain with your coffee and have a pretty strong digestive system, there's no more coffee in the Great Outdoors today.

Narrow the selection down to the metal or similar indestructible material CSDs. Let's consider size now. Take into account your coffee needs. Two cups? Wimp. Three cups? Rookie. Ten cups? Expert and maybe in need of an intervention! Don't laugh here. I used to be in that last category until my heart specialist recommended less to fix that little extra beat in my heart. That's a true story and he was right. Make it a reasonable amount and then take into account the spillage factor. Some of us spill more than others, especially when engaged in outdoor activities. Plan for it. I suggest doubling the capacity just to make sure.

Let's say the selection has been narrowed down to metal-constructed CSDs of at least 32-fluid ounces capacity. That's a bare minimum for me. Now take into account the pouring technology. Again—forget about color and appearance for now. CSDs commonly use one of three pouring technologies. First there's the old-fashioned screw top—low-tech but dependable. Remove the cup from the top, unscrew the top, and pour coffee into the cup. These work but have two issues. Real old-fashioned ones require complete removal of the top thus resulting in excessive interior heat loss and the highly probable loss of the top. Stay away from these.

Other CSDs employ a slotted top that allows you to pour when partially unscrewed to prevent heat and top loss. These work but require the use of all three hands. One to hold the CSD while one unscrews the top and pours into the cup held by the third. Note that if the slot in the lid is not correctly positioned, the coffee may pour out sideways and miss the cup but not your lap. Hopefully you correctly calculated this into the spillage factor.

A second technology makes use of a flip-up spout built into the top. These can sometimes be used with only two hands. Hold the cup in one hand, use the thumb of the CSD-holding hand to flip up the spout, and pour. These have a limited spillage factor unless your hands are shaking from the cold.

Finally, we have the spring-loaded pop-top. Hold the cup in one hand, push the spring-loaded top down into the "pour" position and pour. Spillage factor is usually less than the screw top and similar to the flip spout. Sounds very handy. But they can be loud.

That hot, wonderful coffee inside has built up pressure. Push down on the pop-top and it might go "POP" as it opens. While fish might not care, ducks and deer may find this sound suspicious during hunting season. Dependability and longevity have also been issues in my experiments with these. Sooner than later the pop-top refuses to close due to spring breakage. There sits your CSD, open to heat loss and an increased spillage factor.

Maybe you can order a replacement top via the smartphone. But that is unlikely and even the big box stores don't deliver to duck blinds and deer stands—at least not yet. Let's complete the purchasing process. If it were me, I'd choose a large capacity, double-walled, metal-constructed, flip-top CSD in a moderate price range— even if it's bright pink, shiny stainless steel or has cat pictures on it. Now comes the final step. I move on to another section of the store or another store with a full-sized duct tape department. Yes— duct tape. Every handyman and coffee-drinking outdoorsman's best friend. Purchase a roll in an appropriate camouflage pattern. Then head home, brew a pot of coffee, and enjoy some while covering the bright pink or cat pictures with short strips of camo duct tape. Thus will be created the perfect customized CSD for all your outdoor activities. Use it often. Pour yourself another cup. You are now the Compleat Coffee Drinker!

The Thieves Among Us

Cabin owners can be a paranoid bunch when it comes to the security of their hallowed place. Especially guys like me who don't live in paradise full-time. A cabin isn't just property. It's something we've put our hearts and souls and a whole lot of time and money into. The result is a certain amount of angst and speculation on the long trip north for a visit. Some of it may be downright irrational. Has some drug cartel from south of the border made a run north and used the place for a drug lab for the last two weeks? Did Bigfoot bash in the front door and steal the TV for his man cave?

These thoughts are only put to rest when the turn is made into the driveway and the cabin is still standing. A beaver might have cut a tree down across the driveway again, just for fun. Or a bear may have ransacked the outhouse again or torn down all the birdfeeders, again. But the tree will make firewood, the outhouse door can be repaired, and new expensive bird feeders are readily available at local art fairs and tourist shops. Generally speaking, all is well.

Some cabin owners invest in expensive electronic security systems to help their peace of mind. There's a good market for those with plenty of local firms willing to install cameras, patrol the area, and send you updates. Some of us other guys resort to means that can't be discussed here, even though criminals rarely read nonfiction. These are supposed to be surprises should some misguided drug lord or Bigfoot try to get our stuff. Which by the way, wouldn't be much at our simple place. Like I have written before, help yourself to that cheap @#$ %^&⋆ chainsaw that won't start. Good luck with that!

In reality, fears of drug cartels and Bigfoot are vastly overblown and speculative when it comes to cabin crime. Bigfoot aside, the real threat is usually from more local sources.

Our struggles with the local bear population have been many. They seem to be increasing in number and increasingly bold. They never have shown up when I am legally licensed to bag one of them for a rug for the cabin wall and some tasty meat for the freezer. I'm not above a little revenge, after all. I guess we moved into their territory and can expect them to harass us once in a while and add to the excitement of having a cabin on the edge of a state forest. Nothing makes you feel more alive than a bear woofing at you halfway to the outhouse on a dark, dark, summer night.

The same goes for beavers and raccoons. The beavers haven't really damaged anything yet and the raccoons stop getting into late night fights over the bird feeder once you learn to quit putting out bird seed in the spring and summer. So I will move on from them and talk about some of the more exotic local criminals that you might find in an *Animals of the Northern Forest* nature book.

A lot of the crime occurs down at the dock and involves fish we worked hard to catch with expensive boats and equipment, and the expensive bait we seduced them with. There ain't no old-fashioned leaving-a-stringer-of-fish-at-the-dock anymore and going to have lunch before you clean them. Brutus will make an appearance and leave you with nothing but a stringer of fish heads. Brutus is the local snapping turtle, a huge gnarly old beast described as "ancient" by The Granddaughter. She swore off kayaking for a while after seeing him sun-bathing on shore. He lies in wait off the dock like a submarine and moves in for the feast as soon as you are gone. Chrissy, one of the neighbor girls, got in a wrestling match over a stringer of fish with him once. I'm pretty sure he won. She didn't go swimming for a long time after that.

As creepy as Brutus may be, he's fairly easy to deal with. Just clean the fish right away or stick them in a live well or metal basket. Not so with the local otters. Sure, they look cute, cuddly, and friendly as they wrestle and chirp as they swim past the dock. Just one big happy family out for a day of playing in the lake. What they really are up to is casing the joint, like a gang of third-rate criminals in an old black and white movie. They take notice of the minnow bucket full of ten-dollar shiner minnows, the easy-open container of five-dollar night crawlers and the plump crappies swimming in the live well. They'll be back as soon as the coast is clear.

My dad once witnessed a group of otters ransacking the fishing boats tied to a resort dock. They flipped open minnow buckets, pried off night crawler container lids, and checked out live wells using those cute little ambidextrous paws. They cleaned them all out. When my dad mentioned this thievery to the resort owner, the only response was, "Yeah, those otters help me sell a lot of bait."

Let's move on to the next furry criminal, one you might not have heard of before and who may need an introduction. Meet the fisher—"Martes pennanti" if you like scientific names. To quote the usual sources—"a small carnivorous mammal native to North America." Think of a big weasel, about ten pounds on average or the size of a fat Dachshund, and long and low-slung like the same. Unlike the snappers and the otters, these guys aren't afraid of coming uphill from the dock and raiding the cabin deck of anything meaty left lying around. They've made at least two raids at our cabin.

One fall I filleted the good parts off a few ducks and left the carcasses lying on the deck while I made a beer run to town. Marcie stayed behind, watching the fall feeding-frenzy in the bird feeders. A fisher loped out of the woods and proceeded to carry off and stash the ducks one by one. I did some research and found out they're opportunistic eaters and don't mind carrion. Like roadkill or something else that died and was left to rot. That explains the next incident. My research didn't find mention of a shoe fetish. But one also tried stealing some wet and stinky shoes off the cabin deck. That attempt was thwarted and a lesson was learned. Don't leave your shoes on the deck if they smell like roadkill.

Now we come to a series of thefts that have been unsolved to my satisfaction and resulted in a significant loss of property, funds, and culinary pleasure. I think this crime spree started with the shrimp.

I was cooking up a big batch of expensive jumbo shrimp on New Year's Eve. They were meant to be the main attraction for a holiday feast. A nice shrimp cocktail along with the sausage, cheese, and a little wine. They finished cooking just as our guests arrived. I stuck the shrimp out on the back deck to cool off in the zero degree air. I then went to greet Marcie's sister Cris and her husband Dale and to have a beer or two with Dale just to get the party started. I remembered the shrimp a while later and went to retrieve them. Every single shell-on, mega-sized, fifteen-dollar-per-pound shrimp, straight from Morey's Fish Market, was gone.

I did have some backup shrimp in the freezer so our feast went on. But the mystery remained. What @#$ %^&* kind of shrimp-eating criminal was roaming the Northwoods on New Year's Eve? We wondered about the dogs. Kal, the black-female-Labrador-retriever-in-residence at the time, and sweet old Lou, Dale's Chesapeake Bay/retriever mix were possible suspects. However, our detective work the next morning did not implicate them in the crime. If you must know, we did look closely at their doggie doo and saw no evidence of the passing of hard-to-digest shrimp shells.

Next came the elk roast caper. If you add up the costs associated with driving to Montana and legally acquiring an organic, free-range, grass-fed elk roast, this might have been the crime of the century. I did acquire a roast and more on one trip. Organic free-range, grass-fed elk meat is extremely tasty in addition to being expensive. So the deer hunting crew and I were really looking forward to one carefully grilled over hardwood charcoal while we sipped a beer or three on the deck one evening. Except we turned our backs on it for a few minutes, left it unattended while the coals got hot, and there it was— GONE!

Once again we searched for evidence and found not a scrap. We then considered the circumstantial circumstances of both the shrimp and the elk disappearance while grilling hot dogs with a few more beers. We discovered three common denominators. Dale and I were in the vicinity for both. So was Kal, still the current black-female-Labrador-retriever-in-residence. I was immediately suspicious of Dale given our previous forensic studies had not shown evidence of Kal consuming shrimp. I know for a fact that Dale likes to eat both shrimp and elk. But he and Kal claimed innocence and there was no actual proof. I had to back off and didn't request the local authorities to investigate. After all, Dale is a relative, sort of, and he does provide me with cheap fishing tackle given his employment in that industry. I bided my time, waiting for the next act of thievery to occur.

The next spring we gathered at the cabin for our annual turkey hunting, crappie fishing, and male bonding event. Dale was there. So was Kal, who had to stay behind at the cabin, relegated to sleeping in her old stinking easy chair because a dog can't legally be used for turkey hunting. Dale mentioned that he had made a big batch of his famous Wisconsin recipe venison jerky and would share it once he found it. The jerky seemed to have disappeared into his pile of turkey hunting and crappie fishing gear.

I spent the next morning dreaming about the jerky since I had plenty of time alone in the woods with no turkeys in sight and only healthy granola bars for snacks. I'm pretty sure it was on the minds of the other hunters too. But our dreams didn't come true. Dale kept rummaging through his stuff, even searched his truck, and couldn't come up with the jerky. "I must have forgot it at home," he said. Which immediately raised my doubts about him again. Maybe, just maybe, he had stolen the shrimp and the elk roast and was now teasing me with the promise of jerky as payback for accusing him of those crimes.

On about the third day, Dale did appear to solve this mystery and the shrimp and elk roast capers. He emerged from the basement with a big plastic food storage bag. One about the size that would hold a big batch of tasty homemade Wisconsin recipe venison jerky. It was empty and appeared to have a large hole chewed in one corner. "I found the bag," he said. "And I think I found the thief!" With that he pointed at poor old Kal, half-asleep in her stinky easy chair, and flat-out accused her of being the shrimp, elk, and now jerky thief.

I had to admit that the evidence, circumstantial as it was, was compelling, and likely Kal would have been convicted by a jury of her peers. Well, maybe not, given that Labs are social animals and do tend to stick together and flash their puppy eyes when accused of crimes.

But I'm not totally convinced. Dale might have invented that batch of venison, chewed the hole in the bag himself, and falsely accused a poor old dog as a diversion. Time will tell. I'm going to start watching the good food a little closer whenever both Dale and our dogs are around. It's got to be one of them. The truth will certainly come out if the good beer turns up missing.

Going Home

boot

boat

[bōōōōōōht]

NOUN

1. a small vessel propelled on water by oars, sails, or an engine.
"a fishing boat."

Author's Note—The next piece continues my tradition of giving myself, and perhaps the readers, a break by featuring one of my youngest brother Jim's works. He has lived in Colorado for most of his life. But Minnesota calls to him once in a while . . .

Going Home

So Mom calls me up in April, just before they're going to embark on the return leg òf their annual snowbird journey between Phoenix and Minnesota. The last couple of years, I've flown in from Colorado and shuttled their car back home so they can fly and thereby avoid driving 1800 miles through Before Kansas, Kansas, and After Kansas. And it affords me the opportunity to spend some quality time with their cat, Willow, while listening to NPR and topping out their Chevy Impala at about 108 MPH across the high desert backroads of the Southwest.

"Jimmy . . ." she says. Mom is the only person who calls me "Jimmy," except sometimes my cronies at Cactus Jack's Bar when they've had just about enough to drink, and my daughter when she is mocking me. "We've decided to drive home one last time," Mom says. "Your dad isn't probably going to live through the summer. He wants to do the trip one last time."

Keep in mind I've heard this same grim forecast at least a dozen times over the last twenty-five years, ever since Dad had quadruple-bypass surgery just south of sixty. But it's never easy to hear. I announced right then that the kids and I would come visit them at the lake, sometime in the summer.

Well, the good news is, Dad got better. I'm not entirely sure what was wrong in the first place—some concoction of heart disease, arterial disease, and maybe homesickness with a splash of missing crappie fishing.

The bad news is I still have to go to Minnesota. I've put it off as long as I can but now summer's about over. If I don't leave soon, I'll be passing them heading the other direction on the freeway back to Arizona. Tomorrow at 6 a.m., my kids, Matt and Katie, and I will pile into the legacy of wife Jane's recently departed father, Grandpa Archer's 2002 Lincoln Town Car with Arizona handicap plates. We'll point it north by northeast and hit the road towards the sunrise.

Katie convinced me to drive all fifteen hours in one shot because otherwise we'd just be "staying at some Super 8 along the highway in Nebraska and eating dinner at Applebee's."

I nodded. "And we'd be dang happy to find an Applebee's." Three days, four nights at my parent's lakeside trailer park near Nevis, Minnesota, home of the World's Largest Tiger Muskie, and we'll make a 180 in the Lincoln for another fifteen-hour marathon back to the Colorado mountains.

We won't need a map. You just drive east on I-80 for, oh, about half of a lifetime. There's one curve at about Grand Island, Nebraska. You have to watch out for it. It sneaks up on you. At Omaha, you take a left, and drive another half of a lifetime until you almost get to Fargo. Yes, that Fargo. You turn northeast somewhere near Rothsay, Home of the World's Largest Prairie Chicken. Stay on that road until you see, in order, the World's largest Pelican, the World's Largest Loon, and the World's Largest

Turkey. You've gone too far if you see Not Quite the World's Largest Statues of Paul Bunyan and Babe the Blue Ox there in Bemidji. No, I'm not kidding. And yes, I could go on forever like this.

I don't know why I'm bothering to bring my guitar. Katie won't let me play it within earshot and we're camping on a lake. Sound carries over water. I'll have to cross the border into Canada if I want to bang out a few tunes.

As you can tell, I'm not excited about the trip. Nevis is in beautiful lake country. Many of my family will be there. But we've never had a good Minnesota summer vacation. Every time we've tried we've heard something akin to, "This is the first time we've ever had the heaters on in the cabins in August," or "Usually the skeeters aren't so bad by August," or my favorite, "They say the rain is supposed to let up by . . . the day we're leaving."

Colorado weather has made us spoiled little brats. Plus, you can drive any direction from here but east to visit some of the most heavenly places in the world. All without having to first suffer through Purgatory. I mean Nebraska.

But mainly, I'm just not stoked for the drive. The kids will do fine. The interior of Grandpa Archer's Lincoln is larger than our living room. Katie's called shotgun and she'll pass the time by pointing out less fashion-conscious travelers as we motor along the interstate. "Did you see that girl with the purple and green hair in the back of that minivan? Are there any real hair stylists in this state? Is that actually a perm?" Matt will have the backseat all to himself, watching movies on his tablet, playing video games on his smartphone, and listening to Spotify. All at the same time.

My challenge will be to remain vigilant and ready for that sleepy spell that will sneak up on me late in the afternoon somewhere near Sioux City, Iowa. That town's famous for two things. It's near the gravesite of Sergeant Floyd, the only fatality of Lewis and Clark's Expedition, and it used to smell worse than the stockyards of Greeley here in Colorado.

I'll pass the time and stay alert by reminding myself of all the things I love about Minnesota. I love sitting in a restaurant and listening to all the people order breakfast with Scandinavian accents. "What kind of tooooast do you have?"

"Well, we got wheat tooooast, we got white tooooast, we got rye tooooast, and we got sourdoooo tooooast."

It makes me giggle, especially when someone asks the waitress to repeat the choices. I enjoy hosting a contest to see who can go the longest without ending a sentence with the word "then" or dropping their g's.

I love swimmin', fishin', and booooatin' in da lakes. And going barefoot in real grass. And pulling up to the A&W Drive-In, salivating over a root beer float. And Minnesotans are the best. Like when my friend Paul Olson punched me out in high school for making fun of him and then helped me up and apologized. That's real Minnesotan.

Ella Winter once told fellow-writer Thomas Wolfe,

Going Home

"Don't you know, you can't go home again?" Nevis isn't home. I grew up far south of there, almost Iowa. So technically, I'm not going home. But I love Mom and Dad. And that's where they live. So that's where I'm goin'.

Things We Forget

The drive to some of my favorite hunting, fishing, and vacations spots can be a long tedious journey, especially if I'm short on human company and the dog snores in the backseat, unwilling to listen to my stories. Home to the cabin is like three hours if you're driving something sporty and are willing to challenge the official speed limits. It's at least a half-hour longer at responsible speeds and if it includes a stop for a snack in Motley. That's short compared to a few other favorite places. Six hours to Ely. Seven or eight hours to Lake of the Woods. Sixteen to Montana—if you drink enough coffee and drive straight through. Any of those give you plenty of time to play a little game I created called "What Did We Forget?"

It could be that some well-prepared people don't need a game like this. They made a list, checked it twice, and are perfect like that. But, I have a feeling that more people are like me. There's always something that got left behind. Sometimes there's even a list of those.

So let's play the game. It starts like this. First drive a significant distance away from your starting point. Home for instance. Wait for an hour, maybe two before starting to play. It must be far enough that there is no turning back unless the thing you forgot is something like leaving the campfire on in the living room or a kid or a dog roaming in the backyard. Something that no friend, relative, or neighbor can deal with via a cell phone call and sharing of the garage door code.

You can play this game with yourself. Like the time I was headed to Montana on my first solo deer hunting trip. I started the game an hour from home, cruise control cranked up on the freeway, trying to think of anything else that should have been packed into the overloaded truck. It didn't take long. Binoculars! I needed my binoculars to help scan the wide-open Montana prairies for deer. But were they back home or at the cabin? Rather than turn around and add two hours to the long trip, I detoured past the cabin in hopes they were there. Nope. So I pulled into a sporting goods store in Fargo, whipped out my credit card, hoped it wasn't already maxed out, and got a new pair. That was an added expense to my tight budget but at least they were a better pair than the forgotten ones and were on sale.

The game is more fun if you have at least one other person to play with and have several minds working on a list of critical items that somebody else was supposed to pack. A prime example here is what happened on the first-ever western hunting trip I took fresh out of college some forty years ago. Three of us young hopeful hunters had packed just about all the hunting gear we owned into an SUV and were rolling down the highway to South Dakota's Black Hills. About six hours into the twelve-hour trip, we ran low on music and coffee and started listing things we had bought for this big occasion. Kim mentioned, actually bragged a little bit, that he had spent some hard-earned funds on a telescopic sight for his rifle, something that Scott and I did not have due to our low economic status. But then he suddenly cut his bragging off and stated rooting around in all that gear packed in the back of the SUV.

He finally sat back and admitted—"I left my gun back home." Yes, he was headed out on a hunting trip of a lifetime and had forgotten his rifle with newly purchased expensive telescopic sight. It was safely tucked behind the front door back home where its obvious presence meant it would not be forgotten. Luckily we had a spare gun packed away so this wasn't a catastrophic error, just one that meant Kim was the butt of many friendly jokes for the rest of the trip. At least until he bagged a nice buck with the spare gun and then turned the tables on us.

More recently, my brother-in-law Dale and I play the game every year on the way to Canada for our Lake of the Woods fishing trip. We leave his house in the piney woods at daybreak, pulling his boat, and enjoying the sunrise with a fresh cup of coffee. We start playing "What Did We Forget?" somewhere before Bemidji. Bemidji is the last stop for affordable and well-stocked shopping on our route to Canada. We better remember we forgot "IT" or we are going to have to live without "IT," or pay dearly for "IT" in the wilds of Canada. If they have "IT" in the wilds of Canada.

The game has proved that every stinking year there's going to be something that got left behind. I will admit that often I'm the loser of the game. The list of items I have forgotten grows nearly every year. Sometimes it's not even fishing gear. Things like my current unexpired passport. My driver's license. A camera, even though I have been the official fishing trip photographer for many years. Some aren't necessarily my fault. Like the first year, when I forgot to pack a life jacket, but didn't really care because I figured Dale would have multiple spares packed away in the spacious holds of his fancy boat.

At least I thought to ask, as we played "What Did I Forget?" just south of Bemidji. "You've got spare life jackets, don't you?" I asked Dale. "I left mine at home."

He looked surprised. "Why would I have extra life jackets? I've got mine. They just take up space."

So there's a lesson on rules of this game. Ask the obvious and ask it early. You just never know when that old, wise saying about the word "assume" is going to come true.

I am happy to report that it isn't just me that forgets stuff on these trips. Last year Dale and I were unpacking the gear from the truck and repacking it into the boat once we arrived in Canada. We were about to leave this bit of civilization and head twenty-five miles or so by boat into deep wilderness where there ain't no stores and you make do with what you remembered.

I noticed one large item missing. "Dale," I asked, "where is your big, fancy landing net?" I asked this because I'm always tripping over his big, fancy landing net in the boat and swearing at it until we need it to land a big, fancy fish. It's hard to miss, and also, along with other fishing gear, he actually sells big, fancy landing nets for a living.

The question got him thinking and he didn't have

to think much. He shook his head and admitted: "It's back home, hanging on the garage wall. It takes up too much space to leave it in the boat."

Now if there is an important accessory to have along in your fishing gear in Canada, it's a big, fancy landing net. You are there to catch big mean fish that will not fit in a cheap little landing net and will tear it apart if you try. We looked at options. The outfitter had a few old small cheap nets that other fishermen had left behind in disgust. But nothing like what we were going to need for the trophy-sized walleyes, northern pike, and muskies we would be tangling with.

So Dale drove off to the one small expensive sporting goods store in the area and paid Canadian-wilderness-small-sporting-store prices for a new expensive semi-fancy landing net made by a competitor of his. It hurt him both financially and personally to stoop to this, but we now had a sporting chance at landing those trophy fish.

It was another lesson in why we play "What Did We Forget?". There are some things you can replace on a trip, if you play the game and remember them in time. And there are important somethings that you can do without if you bring a spare just in case. But there is one thing you had better not ever forget. Your credit card. Without that, my friend, you are screwed.

Hard Wood

Hard Wood

There are people in these parts who are firewood snobs of sorts. They will only burn firewood that meets certain high standards. One extreme example are those who order small amounts of boutique woods like apple, pear, or other fruit tree wood, just to get the right aroma from the crackling fireplace on the holidays. Slightly less pretentious are those who seek out a particular wood, convinced it is the superior one to heat their home, not just provide a little ambiance. I met a guy like that the other day. I overheard him ask where he could find a firewood seller who was handling split, dried red oak. "Not that white oak they try to sell you around here—red oak. That's the good stuff."

Me, I'm a little less picky than these folks. I do prefer hardwoods like oak (red, white, burr or whatever), ash, or maple over softwoods like aspen, birch, and basswood. You can't beat the smell of fresh split oak—a biting citrus-type odor like the super hoppy beers that I like to taste. It's hard to beat any kind of oak for heat value, especially when you are the one doing the cutting, splitting, stacking, and hauling and want to make that effort count.

But ash and maple will do, and even softwoods have their uses. There's nothing like thin-split birch kindling with the bark still on to get the wood stove cooking in the morning. Aspen, popple, poplar, or whatever you call it in your neighborhood, can't be beat for a nice non-smoky campfire. You don't feel bad about "wasting" the good oak just sitting around an aspen campfire drinking beer and roasting marshmallows with friends.

In my world, I tend to split all these woods into two categories—easy wood and hard wood. Easy wood is any wood that can be procured quick and easy. Like an oak tree that falls into the yard and lands only feet away from the firewood stacks behind the outhouse. If it didn't hit anything valuable on the way down, the sawing, splitting, and stacking are convenient and easy.

Hard wood is the opposite. It could be that aspen tree that fell out in the woods one hundred yards from any trail. It's just lying there, going to waste. My frugal Scandinavian upbringing won't let me ignore it. I've got to fight my way to it through the poison ivy and prickly ash, swatting mosquitoes and deer flies, carrying a chainsaw and sweating and swearing. Then comes the actual sawing and hauling the wood out, uphill both ways. It will be easy wood once I get it back to the cabin. Until that happens, it's hard wood whether it be aspen or oak.

Sometimes hard wood is both hard wood and hardwood. We have an ongoing feud with the beavers at the farm where we hunt ducks, deer, and other critters. The access road to one of our favorite spots skirts the edge of a public hunting ground dotted with small ponds. The beavers love the ponds and the tall aspens surrounding them. No problem so far—until the buck-teethed, flat-tailed rodents wander up to the property line and gnaw down one of those stately aspens that happens to be leaning over the fence line towards the road. Sometimes they take down several in one night. Thus I have learned to carry a chainsaw whenever deer hunting in this location. This can be cumbersome and noisy and happens so often I think the deer are paying off the beaver and using the sound of my chainsaw as an early warning system.

One night these industrious fellows decided to make things more fun and finally chewed through the base of a large ash tree they had been working on for weeks. It dropped across the road, its twisted, gnarly trunk presenting a formidable barrier. I had to enlist the help of a few hunting partners for this one. We chainsawed our way in, tossing thick lengths of ash off to the side and warning every deer in the woods that trouble was coming.

There was no way I was going to let all that potential hardwood firewood go to waste. The next summer I stopped by, loaded the truck down, and trucked all that ash back to the cabin to turn into quality firewood. I even took a twisted crotchety Y-shaped piece that I should have known would be a big hunk of hard wood hardwood. But it was big enough to heat the cabin for a whole night and that's a hard thing to walk away from.

Ash is a hard wood to split by nature. It has a tight twisted grain that is best split when green and best split even then by use of a 100-ton, 100-horsepower, diesel-powered log splitter. It becomes even tougher when allowed to dry for a year or two like this stuff. The wood fibers seem to shrink together and tie themselves into knots to foil the firewood-making process.

I don't yet have, as I write this, a large diesel-powered log splitter. While the neighbors, nephews, and I are contemplating a joint purchase of said equipment, none of us firewood experts can decide what brand and size would be best. There also is the question of a fair and impartial split of the financing. So I took on this load of ash with my usual trusty 6-pound manual splitting maul complete with fiberglass handle to limit the damage to my aging shoulders. This was definitely a load of hard wood hardwood. The oak, birch, and aspen I deal with will usually split with one well-placed whack and a satisfying "CAUK," especially in the winter and at ten degrees below zero. Cold weather is your wood-splitting friend.

It happened to be a warm day in the summer when I took on this ash with that fiberglass-handled splitting maul, so I didn't have that cold weather advantage. This stuff required multiple shoulder-jarring swings, trying to hit the same spot to gradually widen a split. This was made more difficult by the sweating and swearing that occurred with the swinging. Sometimes I even resorted to pounding in a splitting wedge and whacking the wedge multiple times to force the issue. In the end I prevailed and had but one piece left. That crotchety Y-shaped piece I mentioned earlier.

I've taken on many similar oak pieces in the past. Those gave up the ghost and became quality firewood after I whacked away at their edges, gradually reducing their diameter until the overall piece got to a manageable size. That didn't work with this ash. I gave up on it multiple times but always came back to the challenge, not wanting this hard wood to get the better of my wood-splitting skills, something a Northwoods-kinda guy like me takes very seriously.

I even tried driving a steel wedge as deep as I could and leaving it embedded for days, hoping that some strange force of nature would intervene on my behalf and split the ash asunder. Or maybe even Bigfoot would stop by to use the outhouse, take pity on me, and use his might and mystical powers to do me a favor with this piece of hard wood. None of those worked. I finally got out the chainsaw and sawed it lengthwise into neat triangle pieces. Try this sometime. It's much more work than it sounds and not nearly as satisfying as beating a stubborn hunk of wood into small pieces.

Victorious at last, I retired to the deck to enjoy a cold beverage and contemplate the life issues associated with being a stubborn Scandinavian who insists on burning wood to heat his humble cabin instead of investing in a furnace and a propane tank. This reminiscing brought to mind another stubborn Scandinavian and words of wisdom he gave me many years ago. Wisdom which I had forgotten until this session on the deck.

My uncle Fred was raised during the Great Depression in rural western Minnesota. He was no stranger to hard work and outdoor pursuits, including the joys of making firewood. I now remembered him standing by, watching me trying to split wood at my dad's lake home. Most of the local elm trees had recently succumbed to Dutch Elm disease and were laying around doing nothing. So Dad purchased a wood stove and turned the garage into a woodshed where this elm could be converted to firewood to help with heating bills. I won't belabor the point since elm has long since disappeared from these parts and can rest in peace. But it is a hard wood hardwood that is stubborn to surrender to the splitting maul.

Uncle Fred watched me labor mightily, trying to break up a crotchety Y-shaped piece, probably just to prove I could and maybe even to impress him. After a suitable amount of time, he spoke. "You know, I think I've got a better way to handle wood like that."

I paused and took the bait—"What's that?"

"I know this guy," he said. "A strong young guy who likes to burn wood. When I get pieces like the one you are hammering on, I toss them into a pile. When the pile is big enough, I call that guy and tell him I have a truckload of firewood for him."

I probably didn't appreciate his advice back then. But I think I'll start looking for a guy like that now.

When Worlds Collide

It was an early July evening, just a day or two before our sons and their families would show up for a long Fourth of July weekend of cabin fun. With them would come the hustle and bustle of group meals, The Granddaughter, four mature dogs, one puppy, afternoon floating parties off the dock, cruising on Ruby the Pontoon and, of course, late nights around the campfire. But tonight Marcie and I looked forward to a quiet night trolling Crooked Lake on Ruby, watching the evening wildlife show, and maybe stopping at neighbors' docks for some socializing from a distance.

This weekend would be more hectic than most, with plenty of family togetherness. It was The Year 2020 after all. There would be limited trips to town. No breakfast runs to the local café. No afternoon dinner and drinks in restaurants crowded with summer people. None of the usual diversions from the cabin and the lake.

Somewhere close by, maybe in the big white pine on the east side of the next lake, an eagle perched on the huge ball of sticks it called a nest and fended off one or two mostly grown, and always hungry, chicks. They'd be growing feathers to replace their fluff by now and standing on the edge of the nest, flexing untried wings in the lake breeze. Following its natural parental instincts, the adult launched from the nest and spread broad wings to cruise the shore, looking for an easy meal for those hungry youngsters. Maybe the white belly of a fish floating wrong side up, a stray duckling separated from its family, or even a turtle that moved too slow crossing the road between the lakes.

Back at the dock, Marcie loaded the dogs onto Ruby. Sage flopped down on the floor, resigned to the boredom of another cruise without her favorite ball. White fluffy mutt Kaffi held still for the indignity of being belted into her pink doggie life jacket and then bounded up to the sunbathing deck, ready for whatever adventure this ride would bring. I backed the pontoon out and started a clockwise lap around the bay, with the motor purring at idle speed.

The deer are easy to spot on calm summer nights. They come out of the hot, bug-infested forest and wade knee-deep along the shore, looking for the tastiest water plants, swishing short tails to chase away biting bugs. Their red summer coats stand out against the green jungle, their reflections a double blast of copper-red mirrored on the water. Sometimes pint-sized fawns follow with their own pint-sized reflections. We spot two loners right away. One close up on the shore of Bird Island. One farther down the lily pad-choked bay to the east, red coat shining in the evening light.

Halfway around the lake we come to the real prize. A pair of loons floats close together, out in the open water where pondweed leaves dot the surface of the shallow water. Loons on our lake are used to people and seem to recognize that a boat is not a threat if it's not pointed directly at them. I maneuver Ruby to coast up the shore, trying to stay at a respectful distance. "Loons," I say to Marcie and point. "I bet they have chicks." She swings around in her fishing chair. Kaffi stands up, front paws on the pontoon's low deck rail, sensing something interesting is up.

One loon dives and disappears into the pond weed. Closely tucked to the side of the remaining loon is a fuzzy chick, about the size of a robin, slightly larger than the baby chickens at the farm store in the spring. The second loon surfaces, swims over, and gently offers up a small minnow to the chick while softly cooing encouragement.

Loons are a common sight on Crooked Lake during the open water months. Sometimes rafts of five to ten juveniles and unmated adults get together for a morning social break before dispersing to other lakes for a day of fishing and relaxation. Mated pairs, nests, and loon chicks can be much rarer. Three pairs might be defending territories in each of the major bays of the lake on some years. Other years, only one.

This chick was the first of 2020 and probably the only one given the late timing. I'd seen no others on many fishing trips around the lake. We watched the parents and the little fluff-ball for a few minutes and then backed away to limit our intrusion in their life. The chick was a welcome sight given the gloom and doom of the evening news we'd watched before shoving off. We continued on around the lake and stopped to share the good news with another pontoon-load of people and a neighbor in his fishing boat.

Cabin Fever

We had just pulled away from the other pontoon when I heard a loon call over the soft purr of the pontoon motor. Not the crazy yodeling laugh you hear on a moonlit night. Or the short barks that say "Your boat is too close!" This was the long, wailing "OOO-WAAA" that means "DANGER—eagle in the air!" I spotted an eagle circling high over the loon family. One loon started flapping away across the surface, crying loudly in alarm, perhaps trying to distract the eagle. The eagle performed a tight spiral aerial maneuver, swooped in low over the water near the remaining adult, and then leisurely flapped away down the shore and off over the trees towards the next lake.

We were not close enough to see if the eagle had struck with its swoop. But I assumed the worst. A few minutes before, I would have pointed out the big beautiful bird and enjoyed it soaring with white head shining in the sun. Now I swore as it flew away. The occupants of the other pontoon joined in, louder and more profane.

We slowly motored over to confirm our fears. One parent loon sat still, mirrored in the calm water, seemingly stunned by the happenings. The other beat its wings on the water for several minutes, crying out loudly in a display that we humans could only interpret as grief and frustration. The chick was gone, an opportunistic meal for the eagle or its young.

As an outdoorsman and a Naturalist, I'm used to seeing nature at work. Young fawns following mother does. Bird parents working tirelessly to feed a nest-full of hungry fledglings. Hawks plunging out of the air to snatch a colorful song bird off a bird feeder. A rabbit shrieking its death cry on a dark night while in the clutches of a fox or owl. I even cause death directly as a hunter and a fisherman. And we lake dwellers have all noticed loon chicks going missing before. Here one day, gone tomorrow, likely meeting the same fate as this one.

But somehow this was different. We had just discovered some small hope, some glimmer of normalcy in the midst of a pandemic, political strife, and social unrest. Then suddenly that hope, that welcome distraction from worldly troubles, that fuzzy innocent little loon chick, was snatched away as we watched.

This incident seemed to bring a host of hidden, underlying emotions and fears to the surface. "Stuff" that had been lying latent in the back of our minds despite the fact that all this turmoil in the world had not yet touched close to home for our family. Let's just say there were tears shed, more angry words directed at eagles, and sorrow for the loon parents who seemed to grieve with us. We motored back to the dock, the innocence and quiet of a night on the lake shattered and no longer able to be enjoyed.

This story could end right here, just another incident in a year that had little good news and so much bad. Luckily it doesn't.

About a week later, with the busy weekend behind us, Marcie, the dogs, and I once again backed the pontoon away from the dock for an evening cruise. I noticed a pair of loons up the shore, floating close together at the weed line, in the shadows of the big pines near the shore of an island. They spread apart slightly as the pontoon sailed closer. There, close to the tail of an adult, was another fuzzy chick, so small it must have hatched just days ago.

Where this family came from was a mystery. Loons are very territorial about nesting areas and don't tolerate multiple nests in the same bay. They will literally defend a chosen territory to the death. But here was another family, perhaps having moved to this prime territory from a smaller bay after the unfortunate pair lost their chick and moved on. Whatever the case, emotions were once again high on Ruby the Pontoon, and this time we celebrated. Mother Nature had taken something away and now appeared to have given something back.

Forgive me, I don't normally do this. It goes against the formal training I have had as a biologist and a Naturalist. I named this little loon. In this case it seemed appropriate. From that night on, despite not knowing its fate or its gender, I referred to the young loon as "Hope." Maybe a bit corny. Maybe a cliché. Maybe just plain dumb. I did it.

This loon chick brought hope that some things were still right in the world when plenty was going bad. But what surprised me more was the worry, anxiety, and concern that also came with it. I'd seen one innocent chick snatched away. I didn't want to see that again. Not in 2020 anyway.

I found myself paying more attention to this chick than others in previous years. Looking for it whenever down at the dock or out on the lake. Worrying when I didn't quickly find it and the parents. Concerned whenever the parents seemed to venture too far away, leaving it exposed. I worried every time I heard a loon cry out the "OOO-WAAA" eagle alarm from far out in the lake, even if I was relaxing on the deck of the cabin. My mind would replay that sad moment from early July, see once again an eagle spiraling in the sky and swooping in.

On the good side, I also noticed a new attention to detail in my observations of this loon's life. I watched for signs of progress, little things not noticed with others in years when they had been taken for granted. Things that gave hope that this one was growing, learning, and might make the fall migration in late October as the lake froze.

By early August, Hope was diving underwater for brief moments. The parents seemed to force this progress as the weeks went by. Instead of popping to the surface, cooing, and swimming over to hand off a minnow beak to beak, they started teasing Hope. One would surface with a small fish and wait for the youngster to swim over. The adult would then turn away and dive without stuffing the fishy meal into the chick's beak. They seemed to be encouraging it to dive with them and learn the way of the loon.

Around the beginning of September, one adult disappeared for long periods of time, gone foraging for itself or taking a break from the rigors of parenting. It was rare to see the family together as a threesome. By this time Hope had grown to nearly the same size as the parents and had shed the fuzzy down for the silver gray feathers of a juvenile. By the middle of September, Hope's slim shape was often seen swimming across the bay alone, a solitary vulnerable figure in my mind.

One incident reinforced these fears. I was sitting comfortably in my Captain's chair on the pontoon, when I noticed Hope alone, swimming out from shore. It swam close to the pontoon while meowing off-key like a cat and looking to the sky. I looked up and saw the large coal black figure of a juvenile bald eagle passing over. The eagle continued on without diving to attack, perhaps maybe intimidated by the pontoon or maybe knowing that Hope was alert and wouldn't be an easy target.

That moment underscored how tough life is out there on the lake, in the woods, and the rest of the natural world. On average, I might spend only a few hours a day on the lake. Yet in those relatively few hours, I had witnessed two moments of life and death interaction between eagles and loons. Hope, and all the other critters, are out there night and day, surviving or not. It's a tough, challenging life.

Adult loons usually disappear from Crooked Lake in late September. While they may be model parents during the summer, they migrate alone and leave any offspring to suddenly fend for themselves. This year I seemed to witness a critical moment in this cycle of loon life. I was headed back to the dock, returning from an early morning duck hunt. Two loons had been swimming and diving near one of the islands. As I motored past, I identified the slim gray silhouette of Hope and a darker bulkier adult. Hope took off, flapping wings on water, gradually lifting off for a low level flight around the half-mile-wide bay before gliding back to a landing. I celebrated this first flight and noted it in the cabin journal. The next morning the adult was gone, apparently off on the annual 1,600-mile migration to the Gulf of Mexico.

When I returned to the cabin in early October, Hope was gone too. I don't know where. Perhaps finally succumbing to an eagle or one of the other predators that make meals of loons. However, I have noticed that juvenile loons hatched on other lakes sometimes move to Crooked Lake after their parents migrate. They show up and paddle around with the resident juveniles, sometimes swimming into my duck decoys as if lonely and looking for company. It's very possible Hope took a short flight to any one of the other three lakes that are just a narrow peninsula away, testing wings or looking for company.

That mystery may have been solved several weeks later. My neighbor Tom and I were duck hunting on Stony Point when loon calls came from the next lake just after sunrise. Soon after, a single gray loon passed overhead, circled the lake, and did a spiral glide down, ending with a perfect sliding landing that any float-plane pilot would have been proud of.

Was it Hope doing one last "good-bye" flyby? One last check of the home territory before moving on? In any case, it was the last loon sighting of 2020. The loon was gone the next day.

For lack of other words, and again at the risk of sounding cliché, the sighting did give us hope. There was at least one juvenile loon headed south from Crooked Lake. There was hope that at least one loon would make its way back next spring, arriving as soon as there was a sliver of open water to swim and fish in. And to make those crazy, wild loon calls on moonlit nights to help us move on from The Year 2020.